i

When I Grow Up I'll Be a SEDUCER

ALEXIS EYONDI

SELECTMALL PUBLISHING

SELECTMALL PUBLISHING, 51 Clifton Avenue, # C1802, Newark, NJ 07104 USA

selectmalloffice@gmail.com

Summary: At the age of five, Aphroz's fascination with women emerged. The young African boy embarked on a journey to train himself in the art of seduction.

Library of Congress Control Number: 2023910433

Paperback edition ISBN 979-8-9883085-1-5

Hardback edition ISBN 979-8-9883085-0-8

Ebook edition ISBN 979-8-9883085-3-9

Contents

I owe my gratitude to Heaven for the inspiration,
and to my family for their loving support.

Chapter 1

In all honesty

It began on November 2nd, 2016, in a classroom of the prestigious St. Paul's School in Concord, New Hampshire, where I work as a janitor. Mrs. Leslie McGovern-Gill, Ph.D. in History, asked the following question to her students: "Kids, if you had to name a seducer, who would you choose?"

Behind her, one could read on the board: Myths, Legends, and Unusual Destinies. Naturally, her brilliant scholars nominated Don Juan and Casanova, the two dichotomous Western European archetypes of excessive passion.

"You're not wrong," she conceded through a slightly disappointed smile. "But I expected you to surprise me. If you had asked me the same question, I would have replied..." She turned gracefully toward the board and wrote the name APHROZ.

Perplexity grew on the sophomores' faces, especially since her gesture suggested that no other answer could match hers. Some bold voices wondered aloud if Aphroz existed as a Pharaoh or some character from ancient Greece. The teacher smiled and interrupted them, "You don't need to go back in history, kids. I will forever pride myself to have counted Aphroz among my friends. In all honesty, in 1987 during my student year abroad at Cambridge University, I developed a crush on him, and we dated."

"Hm!" the class murmured. A shy yet insinuating smile beamed on the teacher's face. For a moment, she spaced out. But she straightened up and spoke crisply to gain the attention of the pupils.

"Kids," she said, striding the length of the room, "the principles of all human activity, good or bad, are planted deep within each of us like seeds. While most never germinate, some sprout up by themselves at different heights upon our being. It is then up to us to nurture them and make them bloom. You follow me?

"The results vary from person to person, but the best of us will focus primarily on perfecting one of these activities. Thus, from time to time, we witness the emergence of an exceptionally gifted individual, whose destiny seems shrouded in a mysterious aura. Such talented people dominate the fields of Music, Sports, Business, Science, et cetera.

"However, I chose Aphroz to illustrate my point. When I met him in England, he was to seduction what Mozart is to music or if you prefer, what Michael Jackson is to show business."

Her eyes misted with melancholy as the students questioned her about Aphroz. She answered carefully to avoid spilling anything that could violate the school code of conduct.

"I wasn't the sole person who adored him. Eventually, I came to realize that he loved more than just me. There were many others, hailing from the United States, Canada, Australia, India, Asia, and of course, Europe. However, his charm was so captivating that he made each of us feel like the chosen one. So, we never felt jealous of one another. It wasn't until later, during conversations with my friends from China, Germany, Japan, South Korea, the Netherlands, and Scandinavia, that I fully grasped the extent of his romantic involvements. To this day, we still wonder how such a situation was possible."

After a few anecdotes, Mrs. Leslie McGovern-Gill closed her parenthesis. "I know some of my college mates kept seeing Aphroz years after our studies. As for me, I lost all contact with him when I came back to the US. Unfortunately, that's how life goes."

The course on 'Myths, Legends, and Unusual Destinies' continued. In the end, the teacher gave a group assignment to her students to retrace the life journey of an exceptionally talented individual, who could be a person from their surroundings or a celebrity. "Track down the uniqueness of the character, as well as any anecdotes about them. Myths and legends are grounded in those materials. Surprise me, amaze me!"

Leslie McGovern-Gill —— a tall grey-haired charming lady —— had never appeared to be more elated before her students. They set about their task with equal enthusiasm and a naughty idea: unbeknownst to the teacher, they would pick her college sweetheart as the subject of their assignment.

The youngsters began by reaching out to various internet channels and social media platforms, to uncover the unknown Aphroz. And they marveled at the plethora of testimonials and even personal diaries that poured into their inboxes from multiple sources in different parts of the world. For confidential reasons, some sources wanted to remain anonymous, while others proudly signed their correspondence. Soon, the information flow required sorting, and that responsibility fell upon Donald, the student who told me about all this while I inspected the dormitory washroom.

Donald was a rich spoiled brat, lazy as can be, driven by an undisguised contempt for ordinary people. He had taken an interest in me despite his superiority complex, or maybe because of it, after I once helped him in the hallway with a late homework algebra problem. Thereafter, on numerous occasions, he sought my help for his schoolwork. His thanklessness left me with an unfavorable impression, but I didn't mind. After all, I was not seeking his gratitude.

Donald's group of students gathered once a week and communicated through email the rest of the time. He said he just Bcc'd me on their work platform and wanted me to assist in his part of the work ——that is, of course, doing it for him. To convince me, he insisted on the fact that, according to the clues, Aphroz was just like me —— from Douala, Cameroon.

That information raised my eyebrows, but I kept my cool. Putting forth an excuse, I politely denied him my contribution, mostly because of his arrogant tone and unwillingness to compensate for my services.

Fellow reader, I don't feel ashamed about monetizing my help to rich students. Look, I moved to the US a while ago seeking better opportunities, as a well-educated migrant from Cameroon. To make ends meet, I took this job at St. Paul's School, hoping to springboard into a role in education. I admit languishing for some time after it became strenuous to find a position suitable for my background, stricken with doubt and insecurity in an unfamiliar environment.

Many students in this boarding school, including Donald, often greet me with a derogatory tone as if they were tossing a coin to a beggar or cleaning their shoes on a doormat. They ask: "Still with your broom, Babo?" I don't know how that horrible nickname came about, but I smile back mechanically and make this prayer my own: "Father, forgive them for they do not know what they are doing."

Why should I swallow their daily contempt and settle for a false smile or a pat on the shoulder, when I could earn some cash? No, that's not for me. I asked Donald to remove my address from their work platform. And I omitted to mention a little something that would have knocked his socks off: I knew Aphroz in Douala in our teens. We even hung out as bosom buddies until my girlfriend left me for him. Life circumstances brought me to the United States, and I had lost track of him.

Anyway, I turned Donald down. That evening, however, I found a ton of student correspondence about Aphroz in my inbox. Bearing in mind Donald's tendency for oversight, I deleted everything. But in the following days, the flow continued as if everything were centralized through me.

Before long, I must admit, voyeurism conquered my initial attitude. I secretly started to follow the youngsters' work and even recovered the emails I had deleted. Their exigency of truth amazed me, as did their stubbornness in tracing and verifying any trail until proven correct. Fragment by fragment, they recreated small chunks of Aphroz's life from letters and testimonials written by people who had known, loved, or hated the gentleman.

For weeks, I obsessed over the information and Aphroz, a tendril back to home, a place I dearly missed. The swirling pieces of his story became the sole companions of my insomnia and solitude as I spied on the students' progress. But overnight, their work stopped reaching me as if someone had removed my email address from the loop, creating a shameful void in my life.

After a few days of going in circles, my mind flaring with eager curiosity, waiting in vain for the sequel to pop up in my inbox, I decided to pursue the mystique of Aphroz myself.

Fortunately, while spying on the students' work, I had saved not only a collection of their raw materials, including contact information, but also some fragments of Aphroz's life pertaining to Cameroon, which they had assembled.

I worked with the same attention to authenticity as these youngsters and followed their leads to reconstruct the missing chapters. After some time, in the wee hours of a sunny day, the puzzle at hand finally fell into place to reveal a clear image of Aphroz's existence. From then on, a mysterious force pushed me to consolidate everything in writing for you, dear reader.

But, please, don't misdirect your praise. This story owes me peanuts as compared to the dedication of twelve young students I knew only by their nicknames, but to whom I pay tribute here. On the strength of their work, I embraced Mrs. McGovern-Gill's convictions that, at some point, Aphroz embodied the art of romantic seduction. He reveled in women, and they responded passionately.

Now, if you are willing to put morality aside and bear with me on a few missing dates, let me indulge you in some benign voyeurism and walk you through certain episodes of Aphroz's journey in Cameroon, starting with the Red File.

Chapter 2

The red file

HAVING MADE THE FIRST MOVE IN OUR STORY, WHILE MY HUSBAND STOOD TEN PACES AWAY, REMAINS A MYSTERY TO ME. I REGRET NOTHING BECAUSE, BEYOND LOVE, APHROZ MADE ME DISCOVER MY UNIQUENESS AS A WOMAN. (KONI)

That is how gossipers named the 2003 scandal which broke out on a Sunday afternoon in Douala at Mr. E's —— let's not disclose his real name. Under the pretext of celebrating the success of his eight-year-old daughter in a painting contest, this air traffic controller had invited over a few relatives of Koni, his wife, who runs a Cyber Café in town. Amid the general merriment, Mr. E suddenly changed his laughter to a severe sneer and declared to his wife's uncle, "You must have noticed that Koni disappeared in the middle of your birthday party last time and reappeared only two hours later, didn't you?"

"Um, yes I..."

"The reason lies here."

Mr. E grabbed a bag behind the sofa and dropped noisily in front of the uncle a heavy set of documents in a red cardboard folder. "She has a lover," he asserted with casualness, absolute confidence, and a nervous tic on his cheek. "A man named Aphroz."

Koni dropped the tray of appetizers she was passing around. Her sweet smile crumbled, and anguish filled her soul in a snap as she gazed at her husband. How had he found out about her affair?

Mr. E's half-brutal, half-bitter tone filled the atmosphere, freezing the guests one after the other in a bewildered attitude. When the last vestiges of common joy vanished confusedly in everyone's throat, the guests inertly gathered behind the uncle, leaving Koni alone in the middle of the room.

A black hemp rope tied the red file tightly as if to hold an explosive content. All eyes focused on that knot before turning to Koni with uncertainty. The thick folder seemed to seal her fate even before the revelation of its content. She realized her husband planned this gathering to humiliate her in front of her Christian family for which she represented a jewel and the pinnacle of dignity.

Despite Mr. E's abrupt and disrespectful nod, signaling Koni's uncle to open the file, everyone tried to keep a composed attitude. But soon, as the uncle feverishly turned the pages of the report stuffed with inglorious pictures, stupor petrified the guests' faces, expressing a full gambit of feelings, ranging from shameful shock to the most brutal disappointment.

Koni's mother cast a furious glance at her. "Had your father still been living, this would have killed him. How dare you violate your conjugal vows and shoot your fornication? Who is this man?"

[FELLOW READER, YOU'LL LEARN MORE ABOUT THE FALL-OUT FROM THIS SCANDAL LATER. BUT HERE, I DON'T KNOW WHAT KONI ANSWERED. I DO, HOWEVER, HAVE A LOT OF INFORMATION ABOUT APHROZ. BEFORE I SHARE THE MOST INTERESTING PART OF IT WITH YOU, KEEP IN MIND, ONCE AND FOR ALL, THAT LIFE'S CIRCUMSTANCES SPLIT HIS CHILDHOOD BETWEEN DIFFERENT MEMBERS OF HIS FAMI-LY. UNFORTUNATELY, I DIDN'T OBTAIN ENOUGH MATERI-ALS TO DWELL ON THAT PART.]

Chapter 3

Instinct & Initiation

BEAUTY CAPTIVATES ME WHERE OTHERS SEE NOTHING, AND I WANT TO HONOR IT. (APHROZ)

One night in 1969 in Douala, little Aphroz waited for his grandmother's usual snoring, grumbling, wheezing, and other strange sounds signs of deep sleep before sneaking out of the house with Kooz, his seven-year-old cousin. Unaware that he was about to make a life-altering choice, the five-year-old quietly closed the front door and dragged his cousin, Kooz, along with him. The two little boys made their way to the district market square, where the local young adults had set up for their annual party. They found a dark corner and hid there to watch the merrymakers.

The party was in full swing: a jubilant crowd of bachelors and bachelorettes happily dancing to loud music, sharing cigarettes and uproarious laughter, clapping hands, having drinks, and acting cool. Aphroz and Kooz started enjoying the moment by proxy, identifying themselves with one male reveler each and taking credit for their attitude, allure, and dance steps.

After a while, Aphroz lost interest in that game. His attention settled on one of the elders named DeGrando. This young man, around twenty years old, wore fitted brown pants and a white shirt opened to his chest, where a small crucifix dangled. Of a naturally robust constitution, DeGrando projected a strong and protective image. Women swooned over him, their eyes filled with either languid promises or heartfelt gratitude. But DeGrando had decided to dedicate this evening to the gorgeous one who clung to him.

She was fully focused on him, and every movement of hers dared him to engage. His hand glided over her feminine curves with a delicate touch akin to a sculptor over his masterpiece. From his keen gaze and caressing grip on her hips, Aphroz could tell DeGrando enjoyed her shape.

Amid the general excitement, DeGrando remained phlegmatic. He seemed to embody the Bantu majesty of masculinity. Even smiles appeared on his face as genuine acts of manhood. At times, he would hold his girlfriend tightly against him, gazing deeply into her eyes without uttering a word, exuding a confident sense of ownership. Other times, when he appeared less interested, she would cling to him even more, as if trying to immerse him in the essence of her being.

Percy Sledge's, "When a man loves a woman", drifted from the loudspeakers, and the young couple embraced with a choreographic elegance. They danced slowly, moving only from ankles to head without their feet marking any step, languorous and sensual movements that never crossed the limit of decency ——except, perhaps, when DeGrando's full hands lingered on the fleshy derriere of his partner, as a celebration of its perfection.

People around the sensual couple remained oblivious to the scene of feline grace and superior allure. Everyone, except Aphroz. Without their knowledge, the beauty and the male held him captive. Unaffected by mosquito bites, he managed not to miss anything of the epic dance.

At the end of the song, holding his chin in The Thinker of Rodin's position, he convinced himself during an internal dialogue that this girl embodied femininity and all women on planet Earth undoubtedly regard DeGrando as the epitome of mankind. "What a feeling!" he thought ecstatically. At that exact moment, he uttered to himself, "When I grow up, I'll be a seducer."

Souls that complement each other, even partially, create unexpected magic when they meet. I love magic.

(Aphroz)

The first consequence of this decision fell immediately upon him in the form of a sudden burst of anxiety.

"Why you crying?" Kooz asked.

"Am not," Aphroz answered.

"Yes, you are."

"Listen, I want to be an adult tomorrow morning. Otherwise, at DeGrando's rate, there won't be a single woman left for me when I grow up."

Kooz stared at him blankly, just as a person does when replaying a complex sentence in one's head.

"What?" he asked.

"I feel like a ball of volcanic magma is about to explode in my chest," Aphroz cried.

"What are you talking about?"

"Kooz, if you don't feel it, at least think about it for one minute. What could be more thrilling than to be at the heart of beauty, pleasing women just by your presence, and bathing in their gorgeousness, love, and warmth? Hmm? What could elicit greater ecstasy than becoming the cherished subject of these sublime creatures' affections, and fulfilling their desires?"

Kooz stared blankly at him, trying to wrap his mind around the idea so clear to Aphroz. "Look, Kooz," Aphroz continued, frustrated. "The universe probably has a limited quota of voluptuousness, and DeGrando is operating at high-speed. Do the math, man."

"The math?"

Aphroz sighed. "Never mind. I am a prisoner of the time, condemned to play with the amorphous girls, all flat and annoying, while DeGrando accesses the feverish elasticity of all those mature curves out there."

"What?" Kooz exclaimed anxiously and sorely puzzled. "We should go back home. Something is wrong with you today."

They left their hideout.

"Dear little Jesus," Aphroz mumbled to himself as they were heading home. "I appeal to your justice. Grandma told me a lot about your great deeds and supreme power. Why don't you sign a tiny miracle for me? I promise, if you speed up my growth overnight and make me an adult tomorrow morning, I will not only stay away from nonsense, but I will also conform to all grandma's demands, including dishwashing chores. I see no other fair solution for my problem, O Almighty! You hear me?"

"You spoke to me?" Kooz asked.

"Huh? No, no," answered Aphroz, realizing he had just voiced his last thought. He turned his face away to hide his sheer frustration.

Back then, we had no electronic games, but dance parties. Oh, how I miss those parties! (Babo)

A s he grew, the contrast between Aphroz and his peers bemused everyone he encountered. His actions and poise conveyed an aura of a thoughtful and charming, yet elusive, character. Many adults coveted his exemplary manners in part because of his usual neat grooming. For instance, he made it a point of principle to always change clothes for recess and never understood why his comrades acted differently.

Because of his early ease at school, the faculty had him skip two grades. His thirst for knowledge mirrored that of a dehydrated person desperately seeking water from any available source. The chitchatting of his classmates irritated him whenever the teacher introduced some new concept. However, like any gifted child, when the subject at hand failed to enhance his knowledge, he found enjoyment in class...but solely with the girls.

The overwhelming distress of not transforming into an adult overnight had faded away, replaced by an intensified longing to gather experiences befitting his age. After convincing himself that girls preluded women, he observed them and visualized the blossoming of each one with all her charms in their mature form.

His explanation of this process perplexed Kooz.

"What do you mean?" the latter asked.

"What don't you understand, man? With one glance, I can extrapolate their silhouette and picture what they will look like in years to come. That's all."

"Just looking at them?"

"Yeah! You want to know what happens at school when I fix a scrutinizing gaze on them? They feel shameful of their childish aspect and bloom like flowers."

"Af, how do you know that?"

"Because they stop playing carelessly, stand still, and try to act womanly. Some girls even want to prove to me they're grown up," Aphroz explained.

"Prove?"

"Yeah, man! They show me their stuff discreetly."

"Nonsense!" shouted Kooz.

"I'm telling you! Some are shy, others are ingenious or casual or, you know, mischievous. But believe me, in the classroom when I fix my eyes on one of them in a certain way, most of the time, she ends up spreading her knees for me. And not just the knees."

"Uh huh?"

"Yeah, man! French blondes, in particular... I'm not sure why."

"That's crazy!" Kooz exclaimed incredulously. "You know what? I'm sure you'll be like Elmo."

He spoke of his youth with nostalgia, but loved his adulthood. Isn't that the definition of a happy man?
(LaMonica) (Donald's classmate)

Gifted with sharp intelligence, Elmo, Aphroz's maternal grandfather, worked in a French company as an accountant, a non-rewarding but prestigious position in colonial times. This refined man of sublime dignity enjoyed a polygamous life with three wives.

Pako, Aphroz's paternal grandfather, mirrored this lifeway despite working solely as a carpenter. His elegance, charm, and energy endeared him to a substantial number of mistresses. Until nowadays in Douala, legend holds that the discretion of his romances experienced an upset in 1950 when a prominent gentleman's bride left her household overnight to become Pako's second wife.

As for Charly, Aphroz's father, apart from his handsomeness, he appealed to women with his lively spirit and facetious smile. A smooth talker, Charly could not help but flirt spontaneously with any female presence, regardless of the situation. He was able to court women in front of their husbands, mothers before their children, widows at funerals, or young ladies under the noses of their parents without ever offending anyone. Despite being a renowned gynecologist, he maintained a simple lifestyle. However, he found it perfectly incongruous to read anything other than Plato or listen to any music besides Bach and Miles Davis. Hence, his entourage often pondered why a gentleman of his stature exhibited such minimal discrimination and discretion about his mistresses. Nobody knew that Tifenn, his pragmatic French wife who could not carry a pregnancy, had once begged him unexpectedly to have affairs. "You didn't ask for it, but I would like for you to father a child out of wedlock since I can't give you one. However, you'll have my blessing only if you agree to these three conditions: you must impregnate a woman I don't know, whom you are not in love with, and who agrees to give us the baby." This is how Aphroz was born, although the third condition took much longer than anticipated.

[BELOVED READER, AS A DISCLAIMER, LET ME SAY THAT
I DON'T KNOW THE FIRST THING REGARDING HEREDITY.
I JUST FELT LIKE TELLING YOU ABOUT THOSE RELATIVES.
NOW, IT IS UP TO YOU TO DETERMINE WHETHER SUCH A

While Grandma had a fondness for all my girlfriends, her habit of confusing their names during conversations often led to troublesome situations for me. (Aphroz)

Aphroz's experiments went on discreetly in his closed world, spicing up his growing years. He had not turned eight yet when he shifted his interest from the girls of his height to the challenging taller ones. While the former would pull down their panties in front of him by themselves and beg for something to happen, he thought the latter ought to have a "fuzzy oasis".

One evening, Aphroz found himself alone with Solange, one of these teenagers, in the semi-darkness of their building's stairwell. Their friends ——the four Foudazib brothers—— had abruptly left for dinner at their mother's call in the middle of a naughty hide-and-seek game. The minute he and Solange were just the two of them, a shameless excitement intoxicated Aphroz who grasped the opportunity to convert the remaining fever into action. He approached the tall girl quietly.

"Solange," he murmured sweetly, "the Foudazibs were clinging to you like Chihuahuas to a Great Dane, but you and I should do it for real."

The young teenager kept silent, but not resisting the invitation to upgrade herself from those previous childish behaviors, she dropped her panties. The intercourse that followed, witnessed only by silent shadows from car headlights gliding over the walls, would have been no less acrobatic or intense had it been between two adults.

Despite its rocky development the next day, details of which the reader will learn about later, this adventure marked a turning point in the life of the charming boy growing up.

He immediately developed a desire to recreate such experiences intentionally rather than leave them to chance. Gaining control of the entire process posed an exhilarating yet technical challenge. Although he understood the need to acquire specific expertise to fully embrace this phase, his intuition insisted that only his father possessed the knowledge to impart those skills. He sighed as if he were an orphan. He knew he could never ask Charly for these life lessons. But a certain circumstance came to his rescue.

I'm sure he has unknown uncles, aunties, and siblings. (BigBreakfast)

Old Pako went to congratulate Charly who had recently been promoted to Regional Director of Cameroon Health. They looked at each other without a word. During that intense, silent moment of togetherness, Pako could not hide the pride expressed in his moist eyes and loving smile. Charly, too, became emotional, reminiscing about the hugs they shared at Douala airport years earlier, both when he departed for his studies in France and when he returned home with a degree in Obstetrician Gynecology. His achievement had transformed the glimmer of hope in Pako's eyes into tears of gratitude toward the heavens.

This time, the moment held a particularly tender quality. The tacit notion of a handover, with a father in the twilight of his life, content with a sense of fulfilled duty, and a son shouldering the weight of life and the future, permeated the atmosphere. Charly waited for the old man to interrupt their silence. Pako took him for a walk around the garden, promising himself not to let emotions overwhelm him anymore.

"Your youngest brother, Sevy, is seriously behind in studies," the father complained. "He ought to be in eleventh grade at least, but he's going to repeat his ninth for the third time because he invests his energy in things not related to schoolbooks. He needs to be... you know?" Pako mimed tightening a screw.

"Yes, Father," Charly answered. "I know his character. In fact,"

"We are getting old, your mothers and I," interrupted Pako. "I have no strength left to restrain or punish him. So, I was wondering if..."

"Pako," Charly intervened. "As the eldest child, I am fully aware of my responsibilities towards my siblings and I intend to fulfill them with the same affection and dedication you had shown as a father, without requiring any reminders. I already discussed it with Sevy. He is going to stay with me from the beginning of the next school session."

Thrilled as a man whose every wish comes true, old Pako stopped and turned to pat Charly's shoulder. After another silent moment, he resumed his walk, frowning.

"However, I am concerned about the impression he might make on Tifenn. I don't want him to cause her any trouble or to ruin the image of our family."

Charly chuckled. "Because my wife is a European, you assume that she would capitulate in front of my rebellious brother?"

Pako stopped again and clung to his son's arm.

"You cannot imagine the trouble he is causing us," he uttered in a tone of deep exhaustion. "I wonder if that's what's driving your mother to a resentful silence."

"I doubt it," replied Charly with the gestures of a sinner avoiding commenting on another one's antics. "Anyway, don't worry about my wife, Pako. In France, people blush at everything, but they can be barbaric. Don't forget, they colonized us and not the other way around."

"Please, son," the old man intervened, half-serious, half-jovial. "I see where you're going with this. Look, I am in an excellent mood. This day has brought me so much happiness, don't ruin it. You know very well that I don't discuss politics, not even in a low voice."

They continued to stroll under the fruit trees, one smoking his pipe, the other a cigarette.

"But tell me, is it true that they can go from snow-white to tomato-red in the blink of an eye?" Pako asked, illustrating his question with a double snap of fingers, his voice betraying his playful spirit.

Charly nodded, laughing.

[WHILE FATHER AND SON PURSUE THEIR CONVERSATION IN THEIR CASUAL AND FRIENDLY TONE, SURROUNDED BY THICK VOLUTES OF SMOKE, LET ME INTRODUCE YOU TO SEVY BEFORE HE MOVES TO HIS ELDEST BROTHER'S HOUSE...ALONGSIDE PETULANT APHROZ.]

Sevy had a lot to offer. However, unlike me, he was driven more by his addiction to sex than by his feelings.

(Aphroz)

While some youngsters display their enthusiasm for sports, others wholeheartedly dedicate themselves to artistic hobbies. Sevy, the youngest brother of Charly, centered his personality around a single subject: girls. He idolized them. He also had a weakness for music, as well as Buddhist and esoteric books like those written by Lobsang Rampa. Yet, he directed his attitudes and actions toward pursuing sexual favors.

During his ninth-grade year, Sevy embarked on a clandestine affair with his English teacher, a fiery redhead from Canada who was married to a British diplomat. Under the guise of private lessons, she would receive Sevy at their official residence. The affair continued for several weeks until she discovered Sevy boasting about it to one of her household staff, known for occasional sarcasm. Realizing that she was jeopardizing the Crown's honor, she abruptly ended the private lessons, just before Sevy's reputation as a heartthrob took an unexpected turn, thanks to a student named Marie-Louise.

Marie-Louise, a young girl of angelic character, began skipping school and spending more time outside. Eventually, her influential father learned about her romance with Sevy. After an unsuccessful attempt to guide her back to the respectable habits of their family, he resorted to forceful measures to halt their love story. He used his connections with a police chief to manipulate the officers and keep Sevy away from Marie-Louise. The next morning, a few officers arrested Sevy on false pretenses and brought him to the police station for an early morning punishment known as 'breakfast,' which involved severe whipping for alleged law offenders.

As news of Sevy's arrest spread through the crowd, Marie-Louise, still wearing her housecoat and barefoot, raced to the police station. A swarm of curious and excited youngsters had already gathered, eagerly discussing Sevy's agonizing screams. In front of this crowd, the lovesick girl clung desperately to the closed fence, her heart-wrenching cries harmonizing with the audible wails emanating from inside.

This punishment solidified Sevy's reputation as "the seducer feared by fathers of maidens." Even without knowing him personally, people began to talk about him, spreading rumors of his potential romances to the extent that he gained widespread influence over teenagers. They sought his advice on courting techniques and dubbed him "El Don," drawing parallels to both Don Corleone and Don Juan. His words carried weight, and he quickly became a sort of godfather of organized gallantry. By today's standards, he would have gone viral, amassed followers, and become an influencer.

That is the portrait of the young man who entered Charly's home when Aphroz, Charly's only son, secretly pleaded for a mentor.

He's going to spoil my wee boy. (Tifenn)

As with balanced nutrition for French children or allegiance to the flag for young Americans, one of the initial lessons imparted to Cameroonian kids emphasizes the importance of showing reverence to their elders. At an early age, they learn that aunties and uncles have parental prerogatives toward them. In this context, Aphroz viewed Sevy's arrival as a providential gift because he saw him as an approachable 'little father' who could answer his questions about girls. On the other hand, influenced by his readings, Sevy came to conclude that Providence had chosen him to guide Aphroz through a seduction destiny ——something in line with the next Dalai Lama's education. So, they bonded over that tacit common goal, one becoming the other's secret guru.

Sevy molded Aphroz's mindset to align with his vision of a seducer and taught him specific skills, often disregarding the boy's age. Any hidden witness would have noticed that nothing could deter the young uncle from the goal he had set, especially since he learned from the execution of his teaching ——like a chemist observing the reactions of his mixtures.

Thank you, Sevy. (Aphroz)

Before he turned ten, Aphroz had already smoked his first cigarette and regularly played poker against young adults —— Sevy's friends. The mystical dimension of things, speeches, and gestures captivated him. However, the lesson that easily spread in his mind was that he ought to display refinement and subtlety in every one of his daily actions.

"A classy attitude in all circumstances," hammered his mentor. "You must focus on charming the people around you with your every movement and even your most ordinary words. For seduction to become your nature, you must work harder and learn to control your emotions. It's a package, boy! You hear that? Let's build your confidence, okay?"

"Alright," would answer Aphroz.

"Now, how can you develop it?" Sevy would ask.

"By immersing myself in challenging situations."

"To face what?"

"Unpredictable but exciting circumstances."

"Perfect. Hindrances will persist, but they should never scare you. That's why you should do what?

"I should prepare for it."

"And what?

"And go back again like a boxer in a ring."

"You got it. And that's the only way to do what?

"That's the only way to create steady habits and build my character."

"Perfect!" Sevy would conclude the lesson.

With girls, remaining silent when a compliment is due offers no advantage. (Sevy)

One Sunday morning, after Tifenn gave them the pocket money earned for chores, Sevy spoke to Aphroz, "Thursday afternoon, I will take you to the movies."

"Oh, great! I know The Capitol is showing a Charlie Chaplin film," Aphroz gushed.

"No, Af," replied Sevy disapprovingly, as if his nephew had just sworn. "We are going to The Abbia Theater."

"We are? What are they showing?"

"Who cares about that, Af? Every Thursday, before the 3:00 pm session, The Abbia has a dance contest for children your age. That's why I'm taking you there, and you must participate."

"Okay!" the boy agreed excitedly.

"Among other things, it's an opportunity to face an applause meter. But, with the dance moves I have already taught you, you shouldn't worry, okay?"

"I don't."

"Great!"

They immediately began a series of rehearsals.

"Don't forget to have a classy attitude from the moment you climb on the stage at the anchor's call. That's when you start scoring points with the audience and the girls. Always keep your head up and look straight at the audience. The presenter will form the couples. Remember to welcome your partner with a light smile, and your gaze will tell her that she holds the title of the most charming person in the world..."

"Like this?" Aphroz asked.

"No, squint your eyes a bit more ..."

"Is this better?"

"Mm...Don't forget to smile. Try again...Yes, perfect. While dancing, ignore your neighbors, keep your eyes on your partner, and at the end, remember to stare at her with a slight nod..."

"Like this?"

"Come on, Af! You're not a lamppost. Stand straight but not stiff. Your attitude ought to mean 'Miss, you danced as an angel, and I felt honored to partner with you.'"

"Like this?" Aphroz released into a movement fitting a budding debonair, self-possessed, and regal.

"Yes, perfect! Change nothing. And remember, gentlemen pay ultimate compliments with a closed mouth...and with the help of what?" (Sevy raised a thumb to count with his fingers Aphroz's answers.)

"With the help of a smile, the intensity of the look, the nodding of the head."

"Correct! Nothing else. You got it?"

"Sure," Aphroz confirmed.

I empathize with the women whose husbands effortlessly excel in coarse behavior. (Aphroz)

T hen came Thursday. The entire population of the city seemed to have taken up residence in the magnificent Abbia theater. The carpeted aisles had no seats or standing room available. The background music and the youthful excitement filled the warm atmosphere. When the emcee announced the dance challenge, Aphroz emerged as the first contestant to walk up on stage, drawing cheers from the audience, and hearing his uncle's voice in his head. 'You are the titan of the arena. Do not lower your head. Look up and dominate the hall with your eyes. Think of the partner chosen for you as the prettiest girl in the world and convey it with your gaze.'

Once the emcee formed eleven contestants couples, a moment of imperfect silence, akin to the one preceding the starting gunshot at an Olympic race, hung over the Abbia hall. Then, as if extricating itself from the underworld, the cry of the Soul Brother Number One ripped the atmosphere. And *I feel good* rolled through the room like a rockslide in a landlocked valley. The young dancers engaged in crazy footwork and contortions, with the public shouting encouragement and gesturing some moves. At the same time, possessed by James Brown's energy, the host beatboxed the instrumental part of the song, mimicking the bass line as well as the saxophones and drums.

As for Aphroz, he executed his game plan: smooth moves, finger snaps, few three-sixty-degree turns, holding his partner's hand at times, along with silent compliments ——all of which his young uncle, seated in the first row of spectators with some friends, loudly approved.

Toward the end of the song, like sprinters exerting their remaining strength before the finish line, the dancers multiplied their figures, squinting at each other, cheating steps, and preparing for the grand finale. Some dancers mixed up their steps involuntarily, hoping for last-minute inspiration, but each contestant made it a point of freezing precisely at the last beat of the drums as if petrified by a gesture from James Brown himself.

Sevy prepared his friends to cheer for his nephew as the host slowly regained his composure and presented each couple to the public vote.

[I'M NOT GOING TO EMBELLISH THE STORY. LET ME JUST REPORT WHAT APHROZ WROTE IN HIS DIARY. 'THE HOST DECLARED US ALL WINNERS, AND EACH DANCER RECEIVED A LARGE BOTTLE OF SODA. BUT, WITHOUT A DOUBT, SEVY AND HIS GROUP WON THE LOUDEST CHEER AWARD.']

After the movie show, Sevy devoted their way home to criticizing everything: the gait, the gaze, the attitudes, the gestures, the dance steps, and the smile. He praised what Aphroz nicely executed and spoke of shortcomings with an air of disappointment.

"In your opinion, will you be able to do better next time?" he asked.

"Of course, I will," answered Aphroz. "It is just a matter of practice."

Geez! We would have learned a lot if only Instagram existed back then! (DaBoss)
Yeah, it's a shame! (Donald)

The method remained unchanged when Sevy, a stickler, began teaching Aphroz the art of complimenting and courting: lessons, exercise, practice, rehearsals, criticism, repeat. His nephew had to apply his guidance in all circumstances. For example, when they were hanging out, he would suddenly ask Aphroz to go up to a stranger and shower her with selfless compliments, initiate a conversation, or offer her treats. Aphroz would repeat the exercise until he started challenging himself.

"Later, I will teach you how to seduce a girl without talking to her —— without even looking at her," Sevy promised his nephew.

"Why later?" the little boy burst with excitement and disappointment at the same time.

"Basics first," Sevy explained. "You don't learn multiplication tables until you know how to count, do you?"

"Hmm," Aphroz admitted. "How about you give me a tip now...as a kind of preview, you see what I mean?" he begged.

"N...No," interrupted his uncle in a hesitant tone. "It's subtle. You wouldn't figure out how to use it."

"Come on!" the nephew insisted. "Just a small trick. Look, this stunner in my class draws me in. I want her to become my girlfriend now."

"If I tell you to charm one of her confidants first, would you know how to manage?"

"No," acknowledged the apprentice seducer.

"See? Those are small operations to execute before the principal one. I guess the girl you target is one of the prettiest of all sixth graders in your sch..."

"She is the prettiest."

"Alright. If I tell you that to attract her, you must charm the ugliest of them and..."

"No, don't tell me that!" begged Aphroz, making a face.

"Here you go! You still need to learn subtlety, Af. For now, let's stay down to earth. How many compliments have you already paid to your beloved?" asked Sevy.

"Uh, well...none."

"And you wish to make her your girlfriend? In your dreams, Af! Listen. First, I want you to praise her to the skies for anything...her hair...her shoes...her schoolbag...whatever. You get it?"

"I do."

"But... do not tell her that she is beautiful. Not yet. Understood?"

"Got it."

"Give her one compliment in the morning and another one in the afternoon. One in front of her friends, and the other when she is alone. Follow this rhythm without fail for two days. OK?"

"OK."

"And I don't need to remind you of the smiles and the stares, do I?"

"No, I have mastered those points."

"Alright. Now, on the morning of the third day, what will be on her mind when she sees you?" Sevy asked in an enigmatic tone.

"She will expect another compliment from me."

"Right. But this time, you will not pay her any."

"Really?" wondered Aphroz.

"Yes! You will ignore her the whole morning. No glance, no word, nothing. You hear me?

"I do."

"You need to pass by her with indifference. Got it?"

"Sure."

Sevy suddenly fixed a displeased stare upon his nephew.

"Af? Did you record all that I just explained?"

"I remember everything," answered Aphroz fingering his forehead.

"No! I already told you that you must take written notes. Where is your workbook? Go fetch and update it. Hurry up! I don't want to repeat."

Aphroz obeyed, and the lesson continued.

"So, on the morning of the third day, you don't know her. But she must see you talking and laughing with other girls. It's mandatory, OK?"

"Noted," agreed Aphroz hesitantly. "But...she will be angry with me."

"Yes, but it's part of the plan. Don't worry. The most important thing here is to confuse her."

"But what's the use of upsetting her?"

The question disappointed Sevy, but he remembered his nephew's young age of eleven.

"Af, for now, you just need to know it's a magic trick to take over her. OK?"

"Alright."

"Now, listen to me carefully. On the third day, after you ostensibly ignored her the entire morning, go to her in the early afternoon with your best smile and tell her you would like to talk to her after school. Ask her where and at what time she would be *pleased to meet you*. Make sure to use those words, and only them, OK? And insist softly that she choose the time and place, even if she wants to leave it up to you."

With his tone of confidentiality, Sevy seemed to select precious stones among fancy ones. Aphroz feverishly took notes.

"You hear me?" Sevy asked.

"I do."

"Alright. Accept whatever she chooses and, at the meeting, start by saying: "Thank you for selecting this place and for coming"."

"Not so fast, please, I am noting it down..."

"OK... And then, tell her you're devastated to see how cold she's been with you that morning."

"But..." started Aphroz.

"Shhh!" interrupted Sevy with an index over his lips. "If you bring the topic naturally and remain calm, your formulation will trigger this exact shocked reaction, and that's what we want. She'll blame you for walking past her without a glance or a greeting. Just listen to her with a confused face. After her last word, and only at that moment, tell her that she's completely wrong because you only think about her. Say that you find her beautiful... No, no, use the word gorgeous instead. And add convincingly that, in fact, you find her the most attractive girl in the school. Then..."

"Wait, wait, I am writing down everything."

Any seduction process mirrors the creation of a luxurious perfume and consists of nothing less than a subtle mix of different essences extracted somewhere else. (Aphroz)

I n addition to Sevy's teachings, Aphroz developed a particular interest in actors who embodied the art of seduction and began to shadow them. The young teenager discovered his ability to penetrate the depths of their elegance, manners, and subtle language, isolating the essence of their allure to imbibe it only, like someone removing the excipients of a drug to keep only its active ingredient.

He studied John Travolta's dance steps in Saturday Night Fever as well as Richard Gere's attitudes in American Gigolo. He analyzed Jean Gabin's subtlety and Sean Connery's moves. However, the most comprehensive analysis he made and absorbed was that of Julio Iglesias because of the singer's obvious aura of seduction and the hysteria he induced in women during stage performances.

Aphroz honed his body language from the movement of his fingers to the flutter of his eyelids. He knew instinctively the impact of each gesture on women's perception, the magic of their combinations, and the precise dosage necessary to suggest an idea of love, delicacy, kindness, or a sensation of refined pleasure, adventure, submission, etc. In short, he mastered a full range of attitudes that seemed trivial but were involved in the complex process of seduction.

By seventeen, Aphroz had gathered an invaluable amount of material and saw the world mainly in terms of attraction, obsessed by the hidden mechanisms of magnetism between people. At twenty-five, he could use all the richness of his learning as spontaneously as his legs and evaluate the strength of any couple with just a glance. And by the age of forty, he had experienced a cumulative duration of eighty-two years of romantic relationships.

[AT FIRST, ST. PAUL'S STUDENTS PUZZLED ME WITH THIS "EIGHTY-TWO YEARS OF RELATIONSHIP" FOR A FORTY-YEAR-OLD MAN. BUT, DEAR READER, AS YOU HAVE CERTAINLY FIGURED OUT, THEIR METHODOLOGY WAS TO LEAVE ASIDE ONE-TIME FLINGS AND ADD UP THE DURATION OF ALL APHROZ'S OTHER LOVE STORIES, ONE ON TOP OF THE OTHER, REGARDLESS OF THEIR OVERLAP. AND THE CATCH LAY THEREIN BECAUSE ——LET ME WHISPER JUST BETWEEN YOU AND ME—— THIS GUY USED TO WEAVE SIMULTANEOUSLY UP TO ELEVEN ROMANCES SOMETIMES. RARELY DID HE BREAK OFF; INSTEAD, HE WOULD LET A FLICKERING FLAME VANISH ON ITS OWN. IN THAT REGARD, KENZIE AND HANNAH'S STORY SERVES AS A REMARKABLE EXAMPLE.]

Chapter 4

Tribulations

April 25th, 2007. Hannah H., a 40-year-old executive in a debt collector company, gazed melancholically at Douala from the back seat of a cab, disheartened by the city's state of decay. On this day, she marked the ninth anniversary of her relationship with Aphroz, the man she loved with all her soul.

She reminisced about their first eye contact in a hairdressing salon. Aphroz had company and she had only stopped by to schedule an appointment. Little did she know it would be a life-changing moment. She left the salon, trying to ignore his presence, but embarrassed not to look her best. The next day, the hairdresser handed her a note in a sealed envelope: "We met here yesterday. While you were talking to the hairdresser, I perceived the breadth of your personality through your tone and paid you a stream of compliments by thoughts. Would you allow me to ask the manager for your phone number? I would like to hear your voice again."

Since then, Hannah has kept this gallant note in her purse, reading it a thousand times. She longed to celebrate their anniversary with Aphroz, but he was away on a business trip to the Guangzhou Fair, his sixth visit to China. As the cab passed the small building inherited from her father, now occupied by unscrupulous tenants, she recalled one of Aphroz's incredulous remarks about Cameroon: "Here, everything rational hides a nest full of devious actors."

He was right. However, unlike Hannah, he could change the course of his life at any time with his British passport, should the deceitfulness of Cameroon become unbearable. Lately, Aphroz expressed his discontent with a disillusioned tone and a distant look in his eyes, leaving her uncertain about their shared future in their open relationship. She felt the need for a fortune-teller.

The cab dropped her off in a bustling neighborhood, and she ventured down an alley lined with small shops. Upon entering one of them, the owner, Lamidou, seemed to be anticipating her arrival, despite never having met before and without an appointment.

"Let me guess," Lamidou welcomed her before she could utter a word. "You're in love with a man named Aphroz, and you'd like to know what the future holds for you, right?"

Hannah sat there, stunned and disbelieving.

"To apologize for my rudeness, I won't charge you, ma'am," Lamidou continued in a neutral voice, maintaining a poker face. "But let me be frank. It's not perception but deduction. Many other women have consulted me about the same man. That's how I know his name. I'd like to meet him, that is, to understand what's going on. How can I put it? His case deregulates my internal compass if you catch my drift. I sense numerous romantic relationships surrounding him. It's a mystery, but what's most unsettling for me is that he loves each woman with overwhelming passion, and... I don't sense any preference or hierarchy. Don't get me wrong, maybe he cherishes you more than the others, but I don't perceive it. Furthermore, despite the affection he gives and receives from all of you, I don't see a future with any of you. And that doesn't necessarily spell doom for you, believe me."

His quick and straightforward revelations left Hannah speechless. "is there anything else I can help you with?" Lamidou asked. Hannah silently left the shop, defeated.

He once told me that every time he sleeps alone, it feels weird. (Linda-Marie)

Hannah, bewildered, frantically speculated on Aphroz's potential affairs, an exhausting scaffolding of hypotheses. After much wavering, she decided to exploit her lover's absence to get information from Linda-Marie, his assistant, with whom she often joked when visiting Aphroz at his office. "There are no better witnesses than an assistant's eyes and ears," she thought.

Linda-Marie, a dynamic and cunning young woman with tomboy manners, proved herself far from maneuverable. Some years ago, she convinced Aphroz, using a respectful but direct tone, to adapt his ethics to local realities regarding corruption. "Sir, that's our system. Unless we provide hush money to every person in the command chain, we won't sell any of our laboratory solutions to public hospitals."

Hannah recollected how Aphroz's business had taken off following that advice when she entered Linda-Marie's office, hunting for truth but praying to wipe out Lamidou's bombshell revelations.

"Hello, Linda-Marie!"

"Good morning, Aunty. Nice to see you. How can I…"

"I just stopped by to make sure you and the employees don't feel too orphaned by your boss' absence. How are you doing?"

"Pretty well, Aunty. Thank you. How about you?"

Hannah pampered the young assistant with a box of chocolates, a few well-placed words, and a maternal look. She fostered a female bonding atmosphere and lulled the assistant's vigilance by chitchatting over men, especially over men's unfaithfulness.

"Aphroz and I haven't tied the knot, but I consider him my husband," Hannah casually remarked, looking like she wanted to educate Linda-Marie's impressions. "As a couple, we maintain an open-minded attitude. I know when he's meeting his side chicks, so I let him have fun."

"Now I understand why you never come across them!" Linda-Marie exclaimed, visibly relieved.

"They come, they go," Hannah shrugged indifferently. "And I'm still here, aren't I?"

"You're right, Aunty Hannah. They trend for a while, turn episodic, and pff! change face, so to speak. But you're still here."

"Yeah! Of course, some are slower to vanish," ventured Hannah. "… Like this one whose name starts with K…" A few months earlier, after noticing the letter K repeatedly appearing on Aphroz's phone, she secretly ended up stealing the contact purposelessly in her phone as "K & Aphroz?"

Linda-Marie swallowed the bait and confirmed, "Yes, that's Kenzie."

From there, Aphroz's assistant unleashed a flood of confidences, passed from one girlfriend to another, and reinforced the picturesque side of each anecdote with gestures, mimics, comparisons, nicknames, and theatrical facial expressions. While Hannah encouraged revelations with a seemingly amused attitude, each word of them tore her apart.

The recounting went on until it became weird for the young assistant to tell similar stories with different variations and for Hannah to listen more. The latter took leave with as much dignity as her broken heart could allow.

Without Aphroz's advice, I wouldn't have married my husband. (Anonymous)

That night, Hannah couldn't sleep. Linda-Marie had mentioned a string of women, but Hannah's rage focused on Kenzie, her fists clenched at the thought of the damage she could inflict on this woman if they ever met. Then, something out of the ordinary happened the next morning. At 8:35 am, her phone rang, and the caller ID showed, "K & Aphroz?"

Hannah answered, "Hello," her face a mix of disbelief, shock, and astonishment.

"Good morning, may I speak to Dr. Henri?" asked a female voice.

"There is no Dr. Henri at this number, ma'am," Hannah replied. Her voice simmered with anger as she added, "Is this some sort of provocation?"

"I am sorry... What?"

"Are you calling to taunt me because you are having an affair with my husband?" accused Hannah.

"An affair with the doctor? No... I just want an appointment for my eyes. My name is Kenzie. I am his friend's woman. I am Aphroz's wife."

"My name is Hannah. I also happen to be Aphroz's wife."

A tense silence hung over the phone. Hannah wanted her rival to digest her words.

"I'm confused," Kenzie admitted. "Maybe we are not talking about the same person."

"We are. I'm sure there's only one Aphroz in this world. So, you're his wife?"

"Not quite so, but we live together in my home, although he often spends time at his place," Kenzie answered. "What... What about you? Are you...married to him?"

"Not formally," Hannah rejoined, "but we also live together in my house, although he has his own place. How did you get my number?"

The revelation tetanized Kenzie gradually.

"How did you get my number?" Hannah repeated.

"From Aphroz's phone," Kenzie replied. "A while back, I asked him about the caller ID 'H' I saw when his phone rang. He told me H stands for Henri, his eye doctor friend. So, I saved that number because I struggle with my vision. And this morning, I woke up with severe eye pain and a headache."

"I spell my first name with an 'H'," Hannah blurted out. "Can we meet?"

Our guy is a serial cheater. (Donald) *Bullshit! Not married, not engaged, no false promises. What vows is he breaking?* (PopSico) *Don, if you read everything we receive, you'd know he's pretty much a good Samaritan of love.* (MissLisa)

When Hannah saw Kenzie, she was flabbergasted by her gorgeousness which seemed like a divine blend of three celebrities whose names eluded her. This astonishment led her to immediately forgive Aphroz and question her burgeoning rivalry with Kenzie. It took her a while to realize that the thirty-year-old woman didn't use her magnificence as a weapon.

As for Kenzie, she operated under the impression that a battle of wits favored Hannah. She briefly pictured her rival and Aphroz engaging in intriguing conversations after sex, something lacking in her relationship with Aphroz, but she managed to keep her composure. After moments of awkwardness and silence, their eyes stopped avoiding each other, and the aggressive aura dissipated, giving way to an instinctive sympathy between two women opposed and bound by their passion for the same man.

Hannah started by confessing how she got Kenzie's phone number. On the other side, Kenzie remembered that at the beginning of their affair, Aphroz had told her he was seeing other women. "But we're getting along so well, I assumed he had put an end to those relationships."

"He told me the same when we started dating," admitted Hannah. "And I... I forgot about it. I mean, he made me forget about it."

Both women spoke of their life with Aphroz, including their first meeting, the duration and depth of their relationship, their day-to-day life, and even the loneliness they felt during his absences. As they talked about their joy, laughter, travels, gifts, and nighttime outings with Aphroz, each subtly tried to score points while remaining polite to the other. But the untold purpose of their meeting vanished when it became evident that neither could claim a significant advantage over the other. Aphroz spent roughly equivalent time with each of them, and the gifts they received from him seemed to differ only in color.

While discussing gifts and how Aphroz loved to celebrate their femininity, they realized that Kenzie's bracelet matched Hannah's necklace. Both indignantly denied receiving the ring or earrings from the same set but refrained from voicing what that observation suggested to them.

After three hours of conversation, Hannah decided to conclude the discussion.

"I love Aphroz," she confessed calmly, like a closing argument.

"So do I," replied Kenzie, with equal warmth and solemn earnestness. "I deeply cherish our relationship."

"And I know he loves me," added Hannah.

"Same here. He always proves his attachment to me," said Kenzie.

Their shared assertions served as a tacit agreement that the meeting had no conspiracy against Aphroz. They parted ways with no specific plans but with the vague possibility of calling or meeting again.

[WE WILL REVISIT HANNAH AND KENZIE ESPECIALLY WHEN APHROZ RETURNS FROM CHINA. BUT A FEW WEEKS BEFORE HIS BUSINESS TRIP, AND THE QUIRKY WOMAN'S MEETING, APHROZ BEGAN A SEDUCTION GAME WITH A LOCAL BANKER. I DON'T WANT TO LOSE YOU, BUT PLEASE, ALLOW ME TO REWIND THE TAPE TO THE START OF THEIR EPISODE, ONE THE GENTLEMAN CONSIDERED HIS MOST ENJOYABLE COURTING JOURNEY.]

Chapter 5

The Challenge

I CAN'T TELL HOW MY INSTINCT OPERATES. BUT I DO FEEL THAT I DRAW CLOSER TO ETHEREALITY THROUGH AESTHETICS, AT LEAST AS MUCH AS THROUGH PRAYERS. (APHROZ)

She was a twenty-nine-year-old woman, standing at five feet ten inches tall, whose natural appeal ridiculed other ladies attempting coquetry. From a young age, she was aware of her strong presence and attractiveness, winning every beauty pageant she entered, even those where other candidates tried to sway members of the all-male jury. Currently, she worked as a clerk in a subsidiary of a British bank in Douala, considered by her coworkers as the flagship of their branch.

Several times a week, Aphroz made business deposits at that agency where he recently opened an account. Unbeknownst to him, his comings, goings, attire, and manners fed quiet conversations in the premises. Captivated by his aura, the young lady remained unnoticed by the gentleman. His banking operations never led him to the immediate left corner of the agency where she occupied a desk stationed in an open space, but partially hidden by a pillar.

One afternoon, the beauty queen decided to remedy this frustrating situation with her 'Triangle Trick'. As Aphroz waited his turn at a counter, she tied her high-heeled shoes, grabbed a file to adopt a particular attitude, and broke the bank's hushed silence with steady steps across the marbled lobby. She wore a white long-sleeved blouse tucked into a navy pencil skirt. By the sound of her stilettos on the floor, Aphroz felt a sophisticated and magnetic personality approaching.

She walked with the utmost feminine grace to the counter close to the gentleman and said something to the cashier. Then, she turned and passed by Aphroz, ostentatiously ignoring his attempted eye contact. As she diagonally crossed the hall, with a subtle accentuation of her lower body movements, Aphroz gazed at her discreetly, and the sight beckoned his senses.

Her appeal owed its elegance to a silhouette of voluptuous curves delicately proportioned by her tallness, enhanced by a high carriage of her head. This haughty bearing, crowned with a short brushed-up haircut, emphasized the charm of her face, radiating with the awareness of her seductive power.

She stood in the open doorway of a manager's office, said something, and walked with the same intensity through the empty, echoing lobby toward her starting point. The entire triangular journey had lasted less than two minutes but it seemed to have unfolded in slow motion, creating a voluptuous tumult. The moment she sat at her desk, Aphroz ascertained, to his delight, that she had designed the show just for him, solely to catch his attention and challenge his potential. For the first time leaving the agency, he looked in her direction through the clear view between the pillar and the main glass door. She pretended to be busy but triumphed inwardly, "Yes!"

They both thought, "Let the games begin!"

The dice were thrown.

The seduction game can be just as enjoyable, if not more so, as its perceived goal. (Aphroz)

Aphroz's decided to make his next deposit two days later and pull his 'Back-Catch-Eye' trick on the gracious clerk. At the bank entrance, he greeted the security guards longer than customary to get the beauty's attention from her desk. He headed straight toward the counters as usual. But, right before disappearing from the young lady's sight, according to his calculation, he suddenly turned his head to look back at her and ——boom! —— he caught her off-guard watching him with an outstandingly eager gaze. That is how their eyes first met, despite her reflex retreat behind the pillar.

"Yes!" the gentleman rejoiced inwardly.

After completing his business operations at the counter, he walked calmly toward her desk, holding his receipt as a lure. He waited politely, as she finished with a customer and fiddled with his receipt to keep a low profile. They exchanged a quick, neutral look, and the absence of triumph on his face healed the young lady's vanity wounded by the trick. She gestured toward him to sit when the other client left.

"Good morning, Miss" Aphroz greeted.

"Good morning, Sir. Can I help you?"

"Certainly. I am trying to get in touch with one person from your branch. Sadly, I don't know how to. Maybe you could…"

"Yes, of course," she affirmed. "Who is it?"

"It's you."

The atmosphere immediately transitioned from seemingly professional to totally glamorous. The young lady raised her eyebrows in question, and Aphroz nodded, blinking drowsily as they exchanged the most allusive, knowing smile.

"My name is Aphroz."

"I am Nady."

"Pleased to meet you."

"Also delighted," replied Nady languorously.

"I don't want to disturb your work. It's starting to be crowded here."

"We are indeed nearing the first rush hour of the day," she acknowledged.

"I'd like to meet you outside the bank. May I leave you my business card?"

Their half-intimate, half-playful eye-to-eye contact intoxicated the exchange.

"Yes, you may," Nady nodded.

In their voices, those casual words sounded as voluptuous as a piano solo line in a silent concert hall. For the first time in her life, Nady felt the suavity of a man uplifting her femininity.

A short time after Aphroz exited the bank, her mobile phone vibrated, interrupting the warm afterglow that traveled down her entire body. She picked it up impatiently.

"Who's that man with whom you were discussing?" asked an aggressive male voice.

"Good morning," Nady answered sarcastically.

"My question is simple: who's that guy you were discussing with?"

"You're a prosecutor, but I'm not your perp. I still haven't figured out who you're paying here to check on me while you're at the Courthouse, but…"

"Who is he?"

"He's a customer," the young woman answered, her tone defiant but calm.

"How surprising! And he gives you his visiting card?"

"Yes."

"And for what purpose did he…?"

"Listen," Nady curtailed in a bitter tone. "Don't you think your fit of jealousy comes early today? My working day has just started, so please be kind enough not to spoil it already. And for God's sake, stop paying a watchdog to check on me. I am not a piece of meat. Didn't I tell you several times I hate being under surveillance? Goodbye."

She hung up on him and ignored his subsequent calls.

I don't know what got into me. (Nady)

Nady took the initiative to call Aphroz early the next morning, eliciting a feverish enthusiasm from him.

"I am delighted to hear from you," he exclaimed.

"I just wanted to say hello," she said warmly.

"That's very kind of you. Can we be less formal with each other from now on?"

"We can," the young lady agreed.

"I recognize the bank phone number."

"Yes, I am at the agency right now. My working day starts at seven-thirty in the morning."

"Would you like to have lunch together?" the gentleman offered.

"Certainly, but I already have plans with my boyfriend today."

"In that case, would you like to enjoy an evening drink?" Aphroz asked, ignoring her revelation.

"I would love to. However, it's not possible today."

"Alright, let's forget about today then," proclaimed the gentleman. "And let's say, you're the one who will decide when we can meet outside the bank. Is that agreeable to you?"

"I'm fine with that," Nady answered calmly. "I'll tell you."

After the call ended, she smiled at the thought that Aphroz had not lost his bearings when she slid her boyfriend into the conversation. She also realized he had not asked for her cell number, and she texted it to him, along with the best time to call. Aphroz's excitement grew, spurred by the introduction of a third element in the equation.

When it comes to clothing, leave nothing to chance. (Sevy)

N ady dressed to kill inside the agency in the days and weeks that followed, choosing her outfit as a seduction tool, and leaving nothing to chance. Like Aphroz, she always found a casual way to show off in the lobby. Their connection inside the agency flourished rather quickly while observing workplace etiquette. They exchanged gentle smiles, knowing glances, and greetings read on lips. Aphroz bypassed her customers from time to time and whispered quick compliments to her ears before continuing his path toward the cashier or the exit.

One morning, taking advantage of the absence of customers, Aphroz sat in front of her for a brief courtesy call, looked into her eyes, and whispered, "I feel like kissing you."

A hot flush of inward panic, only betrayed by a slight recoil, scrolled down Nady's body. But she remained composed enough to stare back at him with a silent message in her gaze that read, "Not here, not now, but let's consider it done."

Oddly enough, the intensification of their hushed flirtation in the bank lobby did not translate into a meeting outside the bank. Nady declined Aphroz's invitations on different flimsy pretexts and referred to her availability for a drink in town only to postpone it to an indefinite day. Aphroz began to doubt himself as the gap between sensuality in their daily routine and the lack of an outing widened. A puzzling case. Did he misread Nady's signals? Or was the young woman, whom he considered his female alter ego, seducing him for the sake of the game without any other intention as he often did himself?

The uncomfortable sensation of not being in control bugged him to the point where he felt the need to assess the situation from a female perspective. During a conversation with Hannah, he carefully broached the subject of women's inaccessibility.

"Why would a lady openly indulge in a game of seduction with, let's say a man like me, but refuse to meet him out of her office?" he asked.

Although at this point, she had not caught Aphroz with another woman, Hannah answered, half-facetious and half-suspicious.

"If that man is you, honey, you should know that you project an image of a womanizer. It's written all over your face, and you can't help it, honey." She teased him, giggling and striking panther poses. "Your demeanor portrays an image of a gentleman but also gives off a sense of lust. Only disreputable and even perverse women might be willing to proceed further with you. I must admit, the others may find you charming, but they hate to see you add their name to a roster. As a result, I am your only available prey," she concluded, swinging her generous breasts in his face.

"So, you define yourself as a disreputable and perverse woman, don't you?" Aphroz roasted her, laughing.

"No, as the exception to the rule," she replied, perky.

From that perspective, Aphroz wondered if Nady, lured by his "obvious" carnal appetite, had missed his genuine romantic affection for her and already ruled out a relationship between them.

I always expect the unknown. Dealing with it is so exhilarating. (Aphroz)

To find out, he decided to use his brinkmanship tactic. So, he called the young lady one evening.

"Listen, Nady," he started, trailing-off and dragging his voice like somebody admitting his weakness. "I am disheartened to see that...till now...you haven't found any time out of your office for us to meet and get to know each other. I...I regret it, but I don't blame you. In my mind, we were feeling the same...the same desire to deepen our relationship. Now, I understand very well that...I must have made a mistake. Since one cannot force affection, maybe I should abandon the idea of an eventual re..."

"May I?" intervened Nady.

"Certainly," answered Aphroz, hiding his happiness to have his words stopped before an irreversible fall over the precipice that could sound the knell of their flirtation.

"All I can tell you now is that the road to heaven is long and winding," Nady stated melancholically.

An attentive silence ensued. While Aphroz was trying to understand the meaning of that mysterious statement, Nady continued.

"Are you coming to the bank tomorrow?"

"Yes, I am."

"So, see you tomorrow. Good night."

Her enigma left Aphroz in a nonplussed state of mind. One thought leading to another, the idea of Nady's boyfriend being a gentlemanly masterpiece he could hardly compete against began to stab at his ego. The situation required pulling an ace out of his sleeve.

The next day, he entered the bank with Kenzie on his arm. Unaware of the circumstance, her demeanor left little doubt about the nature of their relationship. Nady suspected a maneuver, especially since Aphroz cast no side glance at her as he walked toward the counter. But before she knew it, an unnerving sense of rivalry grew inside her, crawling all over her body like hot mulled wine.

Ten minutes later, as the couple headed out, Aphroz stopped Kenzie before the exit, in plain sight of Nady, excused himself to her, and walked over to Nady. The latter scanned the other woman and decided to ignore the bank etiquette. She got up on her stilettos, walked around her desk with all her majesty, and hugged the gentleman briefly but tightly.

"I am going to Guangzhou in China for a few days," Aphroz whispered. "I wanted to say goodbye."

"For business, I guess."

"Yes...but also, to reflect on how 'long and winding' the road to Heaven is."

They exchanged a knowing smile.

"Have a pleasant journey, and come back soon," Nady wished him, a glint of promise in her eyes.

The idea of Aphroz running into me and my husband showed me just how sordid my marriage was.
(Anonymous)

Aphroz and Kenzie had barely left the bank when Clo, a coworker friend, approached Nady.

"I'm confused. What just happened?" Clo asked.

"I lost ground with him," Nady answered regretfully. "I'm not sure how to make it up. He's exhausted from inviting me unsuccessfully to dinner, that's why he showed up today with a bombshell on his arm."

Clo observed, "From what I've seen, you still have the upper hand. But I can assure you, many of the ladies in the agency will try their luck if you're not interested in him."

"Of course, I am," Nady confessed, "but all this time, I've been playing hard to get when in fact I'm afraid of exposing him to the barbarism of..."

"Oh no! Don't tell me you're still seeing that vicious shorty prosecutor."

"I am. Breaking up with him is not easy. You know how violent he can be. I'm worried about Aphroz, not myself."

"Take the bull by the horns, baby. I don't mean to sound rude but, choosing Shorty over this gentleman depicts you as..."

At that moment, Nady's phone buzzed. She glanced at it, rolled her eyes in a 'speak of the devil' style, and showed Clo the caller ID before accepting the call. Clo silently mouthed, "Take the bull by the horns."

On the other end of the line, an authoritative male voice yelled. Nady distanced the telephone from her ear as his jealous cries rang out. She responded bitterly, "You know what? I'd like to see you later today. We need to talk."

Chapter 6

Fear

The efficiently oriented atmosphere in Guangzhou gave Aphroz a breath of fresh air, compared to the aggressive irrationality that reigned in Cameroon. During his sixth business fair in China, he delighted in reestablishing connections with hotel and restaurant staff, translators, taxi drivers, and familiar faces from jazz clubs. However, what pleased him the most was reigniting three romances, one of which had originated during his days at Cambridge University in England. A mixture of joy and sadness wrapped his farewell after the five-day trip.

Aphroz came back to Douala Sunday afternoon, unbeknownst to everyone, and ignored all the messages on his mobile phone. He longed for one thing only: to rest from the sixteen-hour flight and three-hour stopover in Addis-Ababa. Strangely, he couldn't open the door of his downtown bachelor pad and went to his main residence, promising himself to deal with the lock later. In the evening, after a much-needed rest, he went to see Kenzie. Surprised, she flew into his arms and covered his face with kisses. "When did you come back, my love? Why didn't you inform me? I would have come to pick you up at the airport. I missed you. Did you enjoy the nice weather in Beijing?"

Kenzie's excitement was at a fever pitch, like every time he returned from a trip. "To start with, I went to Guangzhou, not Beijing. I'd rather surprise you than meet you at the airport." Aphroz answered, amused.

Kenzie batted her eyelashes. "Why?"

Aphroz tapped her forehead. "I love the sensuality of your spontaneous reactions."

Kenzie lowered her eyes teasingly and reopened them with a naughty languor, pressing Aphroz against her and leading him to the bedroom. They demonstrated how much they missed each other and took a shower together. Kenzie wore the silk bathrobe he brought her, as they enjoyed a light meal, during which he recounted the adventures of his journey.

The pair delicately sipped their café cognac from the veranda as birds twittered from the mango trees, and distant domestic noises muttered from neighboring houses. The poetic serenity, the landscape of a windless sea, lulled Kenzie. She whispered to Aphroz, as he kissed her goodbye. "I'd rather commit suicide silently than lose you to another woman."

"Don't be silly, sweetie!" he replied, after a slight hesitation.

For the tiniest sparks of past chemistry keeps shining in the darkness, what we once were doesn't allow us to become nothing to each other. (Aphroz)

A phroz shook off the thought that Kenzie may have meant every word, as he drove through.

The gentleman took no offense at Hannah's cheerless welcome and blamed her tense face and evident nervousness on the late hour. Despite remnants of glamour that still spiced up their relationship, time had dried up their sensual romanticism, once so fertile.

"Let me pour myself a drink," Aphroz said.

"I made a salad. Would you like some?" Hannah asked.

"No, thank you. I ate so much on the plane."

"On the plane, huh?"

"Yeah! I filled my stomach with a lot of appetizers. Tasty, I must admit. So, what's new?"

"Nothing," Hannah sighed. "Everything is as it was before your trip. You certainly have a lot to tell... about the Chinese."

"Oh, wonderful people! Wonderful. They know how to do business as if their country had never tried communism. It's positively amazing."

Aphroz recounted his trip anecdotes. But he quickly realized that Hannah did not seem interested, at least, not as usual. She observed him with an aggressive gaze, seeming to wait for the opportunity to start an argument. The atmosphere grew heavier, and the gentleman bitterly regretted not having spent the entire night with Kenzie.

"Oops!" he interrupted his story, rising from his chair all at once. "What do we have here?" he asked theatrically.

He went out and re-entered immediately with a gift bag he had hidden behind the door.

"I bet it's a silk bathrobe," Hannah answered, a smirk on her lips.

"How do you know?" asked Aphroz, astonished.

She shot a reproachful gaze at him by way of response. When she wore the robe, he forgot his question. It was only then that the atmosphere became suitable for a carnal night.

I experienced the strange sensation of witnessing the fall of my consciousness into a nightmarish abyss resounding with the word guilty. (Aphroz)

The next morning, while Hannah showered, Aphroz snuck a love text to Kenzie. As Kenzie did not reply to that routine of theirs, he decided to call her on the sly...just to say, "I love you more than yesterday." But the phone rang until the voicemail picked up, which was quite unusual as Kenzie rose early. She used the dawn's quietness to work in her home workshop. Aphroz tried for the third time when Hannah came back to the bedroom.

"I know you are calling Kenzie," she blurted out.

The gentleman froze. Hannah immediately followed up.

"Don't bother covering it up with an expression of disbelief, outraged virtue, or angelic innocence. Kenzie knows about you and me. We met and discussed during your absence."

In an instant, her revelation poisoned the warm afterglow of their sleepless night. All at once, words and attitudes that his mind had neither deciphered nor connected a few hours before took on a meaning...and Kenzie's last statement exploded in his head.

"Oh no!" he cried, dressing up in haste.

"What? What are you doing?" Hannah panicked. "Where are you going? You cannot treat me like this...I deserve to know your intentions. Will you continue seeing her? Where are you running to?"

From her balcony, she watched him getting into a cab instead of his car.

"Please, hurry!" Aphroz begged the driver.

The city's slow awakening made his request easier. As they sped through the deserted streets, Aphroz continued to call Kenzie only to reach her voicemail, one attempt after the other. Each time, the automated message grew a ball of anxiety in his chest.

"Have mercy, Lord! Have mercy," he prayed out loud.

He crossed the city, blind and deaf to everything. Sensing his despair, the cab driver asked, "Boss, what are you freaking out about?"

"Huh? Sorry?"

"You looked terrified, Boss. I wonder what you are worried about."

"Please, speed up," Aphroz begged, his voice quivering. "I'm afraid my girlfriend may have committed... something stupid. She is not answering her phone."

"Have you tried calling someone from her household, boss?"

"How stupid I am! You're right. Let me try her brother's number. Please, speed up!"

The lazy voice of a young man answered his call.

"Good morning, Pelé. I am not able to reach Kenzie. Is she there?" Aphroz asked, his tone as neutral as possible.

"Yes, of course. Hold on... let me go knock on her door."

The cab flew through the empty streets. Aphroz stuck the phone to his ear and held his breath.

"She is sleeping," declared Pelé in his typical nonchalance.

"How do you know that?" Aphroz asked.

"I knocked but she didn't answer."

Aphroz shuddered. "Is the door locked?"

"Hum... No."

"Then, go in and..."

"Oh no! She'll get mad at me. She doesn't like to be woken up."

"I'll cover for you, Pelé. Enter the room and put her on the phone, please."

"Alright."

The cab turned onto Kenzie's unpaved street. "Drive to the green gate there," Aphroz ordered. He pressed the cell against his ear impatiently but could only hear his heart thumping.

"I am shaking her, but she is not opening her eyes," Pelé announced sluggishly.

"Oh no!" Aphroz cried as he was bursting out of the cab. "Shake her again, Pelé. Smack her!"

He entered the house, the cell still stuck to his ear. While he ran to Kenzie's room via the corridor, he heard a dazed voice on his phone, "Hello!"

"K, is it you?"

Aphroz rushed into her bedroom, hugging her like never before when she answered, "Yeah!"

Pelé shook his head, bewildered, and left.

"What's going on, baby?" Kenzie asked worriedly, yawning, and confused to have her lover next to her and on the phone at the same time. "Any problem?"

"No, all fine," Aphroz answered. "All fine. I am overjoyed to…to hold you…to see you. How do you feel?"

"Fine," she said, stretching. "I am a bit groggy. I had some difficulty sleeping last night. So, I silenced my phone and took a sleeping pill."

I'm not sure you fathom what two wounded women can plot together besides fighting as rivals. (Kooz)

Aphroz felt the need to confide in Kooz, who had always considered it his duty to provide sound advice, like a big brother. Both cousins shared a huge property south of town with two separate entrances, which they had bought jointly. However, Aphroz went to Kooz's office. After listening to Aphroz's story with strict attention, Kooz, now a prominent lawyer, replied in a deep voice, "Af, be careful, this is potentially dangerous."

"I guess I can…"

"No, listen to me," interrupted Kooz. "Those women are hurt. I don't want to think of the worst, but nobody can guess what's going on in their minds. They are rivals. What did they confess to each other? Why didn't Kenzie tell you about their meeting? Are they plotting anything? I don't know, and neither do you. They resent you and may act maliciously, either individually or together."

"Hmm… I vaguely feel that they agreed to keep their meeting a secret –but Hannah couldn't resist spilling the beans– to let me choose one of them fairly," suggested Aphroz.

"And, from that perspective, the other would vanish into thin air just like that out of fairness? Nonsense. No, no, no. If you set your sights on either one, you could hurt the other one. Will you bring yourself to make one of them suffer? No, I know you. Unless you conceal sound reasons for breaking up. Do you?"

"I must say I don't," admitted Aphroz. "I'd rather have one of them take the initiative to dump me."

"It won't happen, Af! The way I see things here, neither of them is ready to lose you to the other. Listen, unless you're willing to risk a remake of Diabolique, you need to focus on damage control. Talk to each of them and tell them that you need time and space for yourself to step back. I want to hear from you that you'll do that."

"I will distance myself," promised Aphroz, frowning.

"Alright."

"But they know my pied-a-terre in downtown and..."

"Don't worry about that," Kooz said, opening a drawer. "You remember my second-floor flat in the building two blocks from here, right? Here are its keys. The place is small but decent and, most importantly, neither Hannah nor Kenzie knows about it. You can use it until the situation calms down."

"Thank you, Kooz."

Holding the keys, Aphroz shook his head and took a deep breath.

"What?" asked Kooz.

"You know, in all honesty, I would have settled down and made space around me months ago if only..."

"If only what?"

"If only I had succeeded with the bank clerk I am going to see in fifteen minutes."

"Oh, my goodness!" exclaimed Kooz, leaning back in his chair, eyes, and arms raised to the ceiling.

Question to MissLisa only: is she in love? (Cuttiekitty)

Nady could not repress a spontaneous leap of joy when she saw Aphroz entering the bank. Everyone who recounted that moment said that even she seemed surprised by her sudden scream as if heaven had answered a desperate prayer. She pulled herself together to look intently into Aphroz's eyes as he approached, allowing him to read in her soul something in the line of "I'm ready for you, no more escapes." Carried away by the unexpected magic of that moment, the gentleman spoke little and invited her to lunch.

At half past noon, they met at *L'Estaminet*, a restaurant close to the bank. The memory of that lunch is not that of a usual first date where people get to know each other, but rather that of an ecstatic moment during which both sides gave in to each other's charm and magnetism. The drinks and menu they ordered were of no importance, just like the topic of their conversation or the meaning of their sentences. What mattered most to both were the sound of each other's voices and the declarations through their silent gazes.

"I brought you a souvenir from China," uttered Aphroz at the end of their meal.

"I would love to come and pick it up from you... that is if you invite me, for example, this Saturday," Nady responded.

I continually sow charm and water it with sensual sweetness. The fruits that sprout in my meadow amaze me. A lifetime is not enough to taste all these various combinations of desire and love. (Aphroz)

The prospect of this new romance, which he wanted to experience fully and without interference, led him to confront the situation of his ongoing relationships head-on, intending to suspend them. His conversation with Hannah did not go without strong resistance and emotional arguments on her part, expressed in a tone of aggrieved reproach. However, she finally agreed to the temporary breakup when he said, "I am not breaking with you, but I require complete solitude for at least a few days."

As for Kenzie, her expression bore the mark of deep sorrow when she learned from Aphroz that Hannah had informed him about their meeting. She held no hard feelings toward him. Instead, she looked deeply into Aphroz's eyes and simply said, "I love you. Don't explain." She agreed to the temporary breakup when he promised not to see Hannah during that time either.

He never stated that the step back was to choose one of them, but both ladies thought he would, each banking on his love for her to ultimately push the other out.

Anyway, the gentleman found himself with a new den downtown and a lot of free time. He filled both with a series of one-time flings as if he were celebrating his bachelor party, awaiting his Saturday date with Nady.

The idea of using seduction as a tool repulsed me once. (Aphroz)

Dear reader, for the sake of glamour in the story, I would be tempted to write that on Saturday at 10 am, Nady arrived at the wheel of a brand-new sports coupé. However, let's stick to the truth. According to the information gathered by St. Paul's students, she drove an old first-generation Toyota Starlet, a dilapidated car that paradoxically highlighted her sophistication. As Aphroz opened the car door for her, he thought to himself that she must have a strong character to get into such a wreck without feeling embarrassed. He later learned that she had bought it with the prize money earned from a pageant.

Nady wore a yellow polo shirt, blue jean shorts, and a pair of white sneakers. After a warm hug, Aphroz invited her to take the backyard staircase to the apartment. Everything seemed to flow divinely, like a scene from a movie, as she climbed the steps, her hips gently swaying from side to side. A pleasant breeze carried her perfume, while the azure sky and the sun's rays caressed the green grass. However, in the middle of the staircase, the gentleman's inner mood abruptly shifted from euphoric to reflective.

Blues, defined by a dramatic loss of desire, insinuated itself in his gut.

[IN HIS DIARY, APHROZ WROTE: "MAYBE IT WAS SATIETY OR BOREDOM. PERHAPS THE PREVIOUS FOUR DAYS, SPENT INDULGING IN FLEETING AFFAIRS IN MY NEW DEN, HAD LEFT AN UNPLEASANT AFTERTASTE. MAYBE AFTER GIVING SO MUCH OF MYSELF TO CONQUER NADY, I HAD NOTHING LEFT TO ENJOY THE VICTORY. OR WAS IT SOMETHING DEEPER WITH HER? I CAN'T EXPLAIN WHAT OVERWHELMED ME. I COULDN'T FIGHT THAT FEELING, BUT I HID IT FROM NADY."]

The pair exchanged superficial pleasantries as they climbed the stairs, while Aphroz's conscience tormented him with existential questions, racing through his mind at breakneck speed: "What's the point of seducing another one?"

By the time he opened the door to the apartment and let Nady in, he had already given up on dragging her into fleshly pleasures or even into a love affair at all.

"Nice decoration," Nady complimented as she walked around. "Close to what I imagined."

Aphroz refrained from asking what else she had imagined and simply answered, "Really?"

Remaining faithful to his fresh decision, he resisted her expectant gaze. He also held back when faced with her parted lips savoring a glass of juice. He held on even after catching a glimpse of the hips offered to his view while she bent over his compact disc collection. However, after opening his gift, Nady instantly charmed the gentleman with her voluptuous cheerfulness and destabilized his resolution with an unexpected passionate kiss, given under the pretext of gratitude.

She interrupted that kiss only to tame his heart by announcing her newly single status. And she finished him off, winning him over when she whispered, eye to eye, "I want to be with you, only you and me."

Two souls had just found one another.

He never laid with his assistant. Isn't that odd? (Donald)
You wanted the gentleman to take advantage of his position ? Wake up, Don! (PopSico)

Although her boss had never courted her or shown any intention of doing so, Linda-Marie had long cherished the hope that eventually Aphroz would take an interest in her on a personal level. For many years, she secretly entertained herself with hypothetical scenarios of their relationship, studied his tastes, and compiled a list of recommendations for herself in her daybook. "Never let Af spend a night apart. Surely a mistress would fill the void. Shouting anger at him equals an irreversible fallout of favor. Never talk about marriage, rhymes with prison in Af's mind." She meant those notes to guide her through their romance once reality had complied with her wish.

When she learned that her boss had quarantined Hannah and Kenzie, Lisa-Marie tried her hand at coquettishness in the office. Her efforts included tight-fitting clothes and slightly equivocal attitudes towards Aphroz, whose furtive glances she eventually caught.

All these factors formed the backdrop when one morning in his office, Aphroz promoted her to the role of manager, entrusting her with most of his day-to-day duties.

"I am speechless, sir."

"You deserve it, Linda-Marie! You're performing exceptionally well and I'm sure everything is in good hands with you."

The caressing voice of her boss thrilled the young lady.

"Thank you very much for this promotion, sir," she whispered delightfully, smiling as a woman does when she confidently awaits an invitation. "I hope to satisfy you and make you happy with..."

"I'm already in seventh heaven, Linda-Marie. The most stunning woman in this universe thinks the world of me, and I realize I idolize her like... like I've never loved before, so..."

"So?"

"So, I want to spend more time with her."

"And who does this refer to?" the young lady asked, feeling entitled to use a cuddly tone.

"You don't know her yet. She is a banker."

The announcement dashed Linda-Marie's hopes and crucified all her female pride, but brought a mirthless grin to her face as she congratulated her boss.

Any man who seduces an admired woman undergoes a bottom-up push of his prestige. (Aphroz)

When Aphroz and Nady emerged from a taxi in front of her branch for the first time, a chill coursed through the street lined with banks. Like a domino effect, news of their romance spread horizontally among the regular street hawkers stationed at building entrances and vertically into the offices.

People compared their couple to that of Hollywood stars seen in worn-out magazines, expecting, hoping for, and devouring their appearances with the same effervescence as that of children watching television for the first time. Everyone ——including them—— felt privileged to witness their love story growing in intensity.

Even today, in the agency, the oldest security guards and employees pass on the legend of their romance. Some of them recall, with tenderness and laughter, how emotion startled Nady and knocked her off balance in the bank hall the first time she saw Aphroz coming toward her with a rose. But few people know that at that time, this rose episode earned her a relocation to the Victoria agency, two hours away from Douala.

When she told Aphroz about this branch transfer, he thought it represented a promotion.

"Not at all," corrected Nady. "Rather a punishment."

"What do you mean?"

"Baby, rumor has it that our love story has failed to appeal to my directors. I was the stake in a bet between them that they have all lost; for in the past and until recently, I have spurned everyone's advances."

"You don't say!" exclaimed Aphroz.

"Stupid, right? You made them jealous. Remember when I kissed the rose you offered me at the agency? One of the directors reportedly interpreted it as a personal affront and crystallized his revenge in this relocation."

"Oh, I see."

"Isn't it pathetic?"

"That a man would want to seduce you? Not at all," answered Aphroz. "The opposite would be."

"No, I am talking about the mentality, baby. At the bank, not only don't we get all the benefits or bonuses we are entitled to, but most women must sleep their way to the top. And if you don't, well, you're stuck as a clerk. Can you believe it? One of these days, they are going to pay for it."

She pronounced the last sentence not like a fake promise inspired by anger but as a certainty written in black and white. She then stared intensely at Aphroz and gasped. "Because of the beach," she said, "Victoria is a paradise for the weekend when you are with me, baby. But working there, so far away from you…"

"Love, if you have to go there, I'll visit you as often as possible," promised the gentleman.

Nady smiled. "I wanted to hear that."

After she took her new position, Aphroz kept his word and punctuated the following weeks with trips to Victoria. There, in addition to torrid moments, the beach, and a nightclub dance floor, they enjoyed local gastronomic pleasures and long walks along the Atlantic Ocean. It was during one of these peaceful promenades at dawn that Aphroz broached the idea of a common trip overseas. Nady had dreamed of setting sail before, but could not realize her wish, due to the lack of a sponsor. She clung to the subject, and by the end of their walk, they had agreed to go to London once Nady would get a passport, a leave of absence, and a visa sponsored by Aphroz.

Chapter 7

Intoxication

Linda-Marie felt ashamed of the unsuccessful coquetry fever that had seized her. The day after her promotion to manager, she gave up body-hugging clothing in favor of her usual boyish outfits. One state of mind led to another, and her disappointment turned into resentment, shrouded in polite smiles.

As the gentleman became increasingly unreachable and systematically referred business calls to her, she took over the company with great ease. Eventually, the customers' command chain network that Aphroz had patiently built up over the years fell entirely under her control. However, those accustomed to Aphroz's finesse found themselves confronted with Linda-Marie's rough-and-tumble style. In addition to displaying arrogance when handing hush money, she not only shrank their unmarked envelopes but also simply ignored the less prominent middlemen. And, to top it all off, whenever one of these "business facilitators" frowned upon the amount of money, Linda-Marie would outright tell them, "If you don't like our new terms, go deal with XYZ Company. I heard they have the same products as us."

"Why not?" they each answered, matching her defiant tone.

Nobody knew then that Linda-Marie had created and operated XYZ Company, to undermine Aphroz's business interest.

Do we know for sure who's the threatener? (MissLisa)

Nope. (JollyJump)

T ime passed. One afternoon, Aphroz listened to Linda-Marie's activity report. Suddenly, his cell rang, displaying an unknown number.

He answered, saying, "Hello!"

"Listen to me carefully, sir," a middle-aged male voice growled threateningly. "Apparently, as a hobby, you sleep with married women. You shouldn't have messed with mine. Hear me?"

Aphroz froze in terror. He had never received such a call.

"Who are you, sir?" he asked.

"It doesn't matter. I know who you are, where you live, and all your whereabouts. From now on, I got you in my crosshairs."

The man hung up, leaving Aphroz speechless for a while. The gentleman immediately thought about Rodrigue, his distant cousin who had been recently murdered by his mistress's husband. The townspeople were still talking about the tragedy.

"Any problem, sir?" Linda-Marie asked.

Aphroz took some time to regroup from the shock.

"Uh, a jealous man just threatened me, Linda-Marie. And...and I have no idea who he is."

"Oh wow! That's serious, sir. You ought to be very careful and maybe cons ider..."

"Consider what?"

"Sir, in my humble opinion, you should seize this opportunity to get rid of..."

At that moment, Aphroz's cell rang again, startling Linda-Marie.

The gentleman's expression bloomed. "Hey, sweetie," he answered.

Linda-Marie glanced at him with a curious mixture of discouragement and anger. Then she stood up and walked out of the office.

"Hey, baby, it's so refreshing to hear your voice," Nady whispered from the other end of the line. "I wanted to let you know that my passport has been issued, and my days off have been granted as I requested."

"Fantastic!" Aphroz exclaimed. "Now, you need to assemble all the required documents for a visa."

"I already have all of them, except for the employer's certificate that our head office is currently processing."

"Great!"

"I must go, sweetheart. Talk to you later."

The gentleman returned to his concerns, trying to recall the unknown man's voice. Who could he be? A cheated husband? A jealous boyfriend? An estranged lover? How serious was his threat? And to which woman was he related?

When Aphroz went to see him, Kooz suggested, "It can also come from a vindictive woman hiring someone to scare you, Af. Your stubbornness prevents us from identifying the source of this threat. I told you to slow down, but…"

"I did," protested Aphroz.

"Um!" chuckled Kooz. "For how long? How many new affairs have you started since then? How many old romances have you reignited?"

"Wait…" started Aphroz pensively, as if a picture was forming in his mind. "Now that you mention it, I just remembered seeing Koni twice."

"What? The air traffic controller's wife?"

"Yes," replied Aphroz.

"For heaven's sake! Why did you… But… Wait a minute… After the scandal, didn't they move to Yaounde?"

"That's true," confirmed Aphroz, scratching his neck. "But they returned to Douala recently. The husband is now an air traffic control supervisor here."

"Come on, Af! Why did you meet his wife again?"

"I… I don't know. She called me and…and started pouring her soul out to me about her problems, her spouse's psychiatric disorders, and…"

"What? Her husband has mental health conditions and he's a supervisor at the Air Traffic Control?"

"Yes, because officially nobody has diagnosed him yet and…"

"Oh, Gracious Lord, be merciful! How can that be possible? What is happening in this country? Oh, my goodness! Do you see? He's the kind of guy who can have his wife followed. I don't want to alarm you more than necessary, but after what happened, rest assured that the dude hasn't forgotten your face yet!"

Kooz massaged his temples, staring at Aphroz in the utmost perplexity.

"I prefer not to ask if you've met Kenzie or Hannah again. But didn't you say you were in love with the bank clerk?"

"I am."

"Then… Pssh! Tell me, have you made a return call to the person who made the threat?"

"No."

"Okay. Write down his number for me. It's certainly a telephone booth, but if I ever discover something, I'll let you know. I must go back to court now. Once again, take a break at least from non-single women."

When I look back at a woman, I pay homage to her femininity. I'm being rude when I don't. (Aphroz)

This time, Aphroz entered a period of full hibernation mode, which involved significantly reducing his contact with women. The only exception was Nady, but she happened to be in Victoria. Embracing this ascetic lifestyle, he also incorporated partial fasting, which made it more bearable and cleared his mind and schedule.

Despite the struggle of ignoring the impending threat, Aphroz found solace in relaxation. He began spending more time at the office and, strangely enough, focused on the well-being of his employees rather than solely on the health of his company. However, the most significant change occurred outside his workplace.

The gentleman deserted his seduction meadow. No plant watering or seed sowing. No bud visiting or ripe fruit picking. No intoxication with the aroma of blooming flowers and no surprise to any Venus. Keeping distance became his theme. On the streets, he valiantly resisted viewing encounters with women as opportunities for seduction, regardless of their attractiveness. There were no silent compliments or invitations to get acquainted.

He made conscious efforts to avoid guessing nudities, intimate perfumes, and personalities through body language. He exerted himself not to linger his gazes on jiggling bosoms, adjust his path to coincide with well-shaped buttocks in front of him, or discreetly examine panty lines. He fought against his natural inclinations to keep his interactions with women superficial, brief, and devoid of suggestive language.

No other description can reflect Aphroz's state of mind in the days leading up to March 8.

The globe-trotters who have enjoyed Rio Carnival or Munich Oktoberfest should plan Douala as their next holiday destination, and make it coincide with March 8. (Aphroz)

In Cameroon, even toddlers recognize the date of International Women's Day, as established by UNESCO. It is well-known that the cities become engulfed in madness for twenty-four hours as women celebrate, all dressed in clothing made from the same colorful fabric specially printed with slogans about their role in society.

On March 8th, women awaken with a revolutionary mindset and liberate themselves from any moral, physical, or material obligations or constraints typically associated with the feminine condition. The most reasonable ladies simply refrain from doing any housework, while the more adventurous ones immerse themselves in activities of uninhibited freedom. If you, as a visitor, happen to miss these festivities, you will hear about them the next day as the city becomes littered with empty bottles, used condoms, abandoned shoes, torn G-strings, and juicy anecdotes.

So, in the two weeks leading up to this twenty-four-hour frenzy of the predatory gazelles, a threat had forced Aphroz to live like a prude numbed by sedatives.

I feel hidden things pertaining to carnal energy. (Aphroz)

Βut on the morning of March 8, an imperceptible scent wafted in the air, teasing his senses, and reaching the depths of the sanctuary where his libido had sought refuge. He felt an unusual urge to stretch not only his body but his entire being, encompassing his thoughts, desires, movements, and instincts.

In the notes Linda-Marie sent to St. Paul's students along with some excerpts of Aphroz's journal she often sneaked into, she made a point to mention this date. Her boss, occupied with important business in his office throughout the day, paced back and forth between his desk and the windows, observing the merrymakers in the streets. His ears perked up at their clamor. "He reminded me of a caged animal eager to return to its natural habitat," Linda-Marie wrote. "Every time our eyes met, I felt completely vulnerable and experienced hot flashes."

At the end of the workday, Aphroz enjoyed a few snacks at his desk, freshened up, and finally succumbed to the allure of the vibrant atmosphere outside.

I haven't learned to give anything but myself in exchange for love. It feels phenomenal to be desired. (Aphroz)

B ars, lounges, and beaneries with terraces on the sidewalks blasted songs that intertwined with each other. Enthusiastic revelers filled the air with catchy refrains, shouts, laughter, and nonsensical discussions that reflected their drinking. Aphroz strolled the district streets without any specific destination, smiling at all the hips waddling in front of him as if he silently conversed with each of them.

The ambient energy guided him to The Tsunami, a nightclub with a decent reputation where the doorman recognized him.

"Today, the place is boiling, sir," he warned Aphroz.

"Thank you, my dear, but a change of pace won't hurt me."

When Aphroz opened the second airlock door to the discotheque, he recoiled at the sight of the supercharged crowd. For once, the place's name rang true. Even for him, the madness of women in this place looked out of control. He moved three steps forward to greet a friend, but his survival instinct alerted him that if he stayed, he would have to deal not only with gazelles but tigresses ready to rip off any well-dressed fresh meat. That thought had barely crossed his mind when a swell of carnivores headed toward him. He retraced his steps as quickly as possible and went out.

"Spiced enough?" the doorman asked ironically. Aphroz smiled back, tipped him, and admitted, "Out of my league, tonight."

In comparison, the hustle and bustle outside now seemed very good-natured, despite the "psst" some excited women in search of company hissed in his direction as he wandered the streets.

He had a drink on the terrace of a packed bar. There, he gently declined to dance with two massive creatures. Later, he found himself entering The Private Key, a nightclub with fewer people than The Tsunami. After his usual circular glance to assess if the surrounding vibrations suited him, the gentleman decided to stay. He sensed the lingering aura from various groups of revelers since the exceptional opening at noon. Now, the place heated up with the least hysterical women of the day. The disc jockey sought to create a warm and inviting ambiance "in honor of the ladies' night".

The gentleman hugged a few friends and sat at the counter. Just before ordering a drink, the first notes of *Sexual Healing* by Marvin Gaye rang out, spawning an ecstatic cry to escape his mouth. He rose from his stool as if answering an irresistible call, raised his arms to the ceiling, and undulated gently on a cadenced step to the dance floor, his eyes closed. The rhythm, slow and cool, became his only partner and lived within his body.

Soon, his choreographic union with that ode of physical love mysteriously attracted women grooving around him. Some observed him and bit their lips impulsively. Others tried to become his official dance partner, touching him discreetly to get his attention. Occasionally, an unknown lady would press her body to his back, following his movements with her arms wrapped around his torso.

The disc jockey reported this scene to the students of St. Paul's. "With his eyes closed, Aphroz appeared to offer himself to the music as well as to those ladies around him. The whole thing, seemingly feeding their fantasies, filled the atmosphere with sensuality at its extreme. I didn't want it to end, so I replayed the song from the middle twice."

When the music changed to zouk, Aphroz opened his eyes. No need to look around; he knew his chances of ending the night with a woman by his side stood high. No sooner had this certainty occurred to him than a mixed-race woman of average proportion caught his arm as he began to leave the dance floor.

"Let's groove together on this one," she invited him.

She wore a ponytail, a pair of low-waist jeans, and a corset pushing up her breasts. Undeniably pretty. Aphroz accepted her invitation. Zouk lovers were all over the dance floor, now dimly lit. From the beginning, the lady started rubbing against him in a more languid manner than the rhythm of the music required. Much more. She probably found the gentleman's demeanor to be too decent for her taste because, in a sudden move, she grabbed his hands, slid them from her waist to her buttocks, and squeezed them there to make her expectations clear, before wrapping her arms around his neck.

Her bold behavior was not out of place on that Women's Day, but Aphroz could not forfeit the finesse and subtlety he always linked to the journey of seduction. So, he started a conversation. It turned out the young lady had the husky voice of a heavy smoker and an unattractive accent that made it difficult for Aphroz to understand her.

The contrast with her fine features negated the hint of glamour in her eyes and turned Aphroz off once and for all. Hiding his disappointment behind a polite conversation, he could only break free of her two more zouk dances later. But in the meantime, he had made promising eye contact with a dark-skinned leggy lady nearby. She assured him, with the silent vocabulary of discreet facial expressions, that the manikin dancing with her was "not at all" her boyfriend.

To create an opportunity to speak to that long-legged woman, Aphroz ordered a Scotch Coke and sat down on a stool, two rows behind the dance floor where she grooved. He had barely swallowed the first sip of his drink when the mixed-race lady came from nowhere, caught him off-guard, and stood deep between his legs as if he had invited her.

"I want to finish the night in your company," she declared without further preamble.

Had she tempered her authoritative tone, she would have sounded sensual. Instead, her attitude annoyed Aphroz. He gazed at her in perplexity.

"You will not regret it," she added.

"Really?" the gentleman asked in an intentionally disinterested tone.

"I will ride you like...like no other woman has ever possessed you."

"Quite a program!"

"Oh, yes!" she replied ecstatically, sliding her hand between Aphroz's thighs.

The gentleman kept his cool, thinking, "Rude and incandescent!"

"Could you please remove your hand?" he demanded, quietly sipping from his glass, and watching the dance floor.

"You don't find me pretty?"

"Of course, you are. But could you remove your hand?"

"Am I not to your liking?"

"Stop pawing me, if you please."

"No," The Incandescent replied sternly, rubbing him harder, her gaze displaying a dominant tendency. "My paw here is part of my project."

Because of the music, people around could not hear their exchanges, but many curious ladies nearby, witnessing the incident, started laughing and whispering to each other. While Aphroz looked away to divert their attention from his ordeal, The Incandescent could not care less.

"I want you," she said.

"I assure you, I'm flattered," the gentleman answered, faking a smile. "But your hand on my private parts is too much. Could you..."

"You know what," she interrupted him with her husky voice, now sounding upset, "many men in this nightclub want me. They're begging me to spend the night with them. But I've chosen you to have fun with. So, don't be picky."

"Listen, miss. If you already have admirers requesting you, please, don't disappoint them. Go for it!"

"No," she replied, unfazed by her unsuccessful attempt. "I will be yours and you will be mine. Tonight is ours. Stop looking at other women."

"Could you remove your hand from my crotch?"

"Don't be a wet blanket. Let's have fun together."

"I would like to use the bathroom."

"Liar! You're just trying to escape from me."

"This is ridiculous. As far as I know, I am not your prisoner."

"You're not. But if you go to the bathroom, I will come with you."

Aphroz huffed.

"I have been patient with you so far. So, be nice and let me go relieve myself, alright?"

She looked at him and reluctantly surrendered. "Okay, but I am not moving from here and I will be waiting for you."

As an essential element of the ambient euphoria, the music was in full swing. The revelers exuded joy as they showcased themselves and sought recognition, filling the air with their energy, happiness, and camaraderie. In every woman's eyes, you could read pure disregard for the future, the desire to inspire, and the anticipated afterglow of their most exhilarating day.

Aphroz made his way through the semi-darkness of the lively crowd toward the men's room when he stumbled heavily into the dark-skinned lady's leg. She introduced herself as Bibi, and a minute later, they were joking cheek-to-cheek under the neon lights.

"Sorry, but if I hadn't tripped you up..."

"Maybe we wouldn't be dancing," Aphroz smiled.

"Does that make me as saucy a girl as the mixed raced one who wouldn't let you go?"

"Since I didn't break my teeth, you're far from her naughty class...Oh, you..."

"Yes, I saw you, as did everyone here. I followed the whole scene with my friends. She stunned us when she..."

"My goodness! Don't tell me about that."

"She plays in the league of perverse."

The gentleman gasped in surprise.

"Say it again," he demanded, smiling.

"She's not your style... unless you have a soft spot for the grotesque genre," Bibi emphasized.

Aphroz laughed.

"She longs to finish the night with you," insisted Bibi.

"And I would like to spend it with you."

"Hmm, you're fast."

"You are pretty."

"Despite my curves?"

"They suit you."

"Thank you. You sure you don't prefer the slim girl begging you over there?"

"I love your style."

Bibi smiled.

"Spell your name for me again."

"APHROZ."

"Where did you get that name?"

"My father chose it for me."

"I like it. There is something mysterious in it."

"If you say so."

"I say so. I can also say that I dig you. But…"

"But?"

"But if I follow you tonight, I will outrage the group of friends I'm with. You don't want me to throw myself in the league of the perverse, do you?"

"Uh…"

"How about we meet tomorrow?"

"Agreed," the gentleman answered.

They grooved gracefully to a few songs and enjoyed themselves to the point of forgetting everything around them. Then… "Let me get back to my friends," Bibi finally said. "I'll give you my cell number later."

After that sweet moment, the gentleman went to the bar to avoid The Incandescent. But, as soon as he seated himself, she appeared out of nowhere and clung to him, just like the previous time, despite the brighter light.

"You should end this habit of grabbing me," protested Aphroz.

"I told you I'm yours tonight. I'll let you do whatever you want to me, you know."

"Listen, miss, I don't mean to be choosy, but that may be for another day, okay?"

The Incandescent sucked her teeth in the way only African ladies do to highlight their extreme feelings.

"It has never happened to me," she murmured menacingly, her eyes half-closed.

"What?"

"What? That a man turns down my advances."

Her lips barely moved. "Is it because of that fat-assed woman you danced with?"

"Uh? Um… yes. Yes, indeed. We are dating."

"That's a lie!" whispered The Incandescent. "You met her for the first time tonight."

"Listen, now…"

"I can assure you she doesn't know what to do with her enormous buttocks. Whereas me…"

"Come on, now! Remove your hand," Aphroz protested.

To show that he was about to escalate the situation, he frowned and turned abruptly toward the white-bearded bartender he knew. "Hey, Tétè!" he called.

Old Tétè came closer to his ear, smiling mockingly. "Let me guess," he murmured in Aphroz's ear before the latter had a chance to say anything. "You just realized she's a hooker, right? Don't answer. I know you stay away from women of her ilk, but man, you don't want me to call the bouncer about a fishy smell at the fishmonger on a big market day, do you?"

Aphroz held back his laughter. But by the time he turned around, The Incandescent had finally unglued herself from him and moved away, sucking her teeth in puzzlement. She kept an eye on him from afar, though. Bibi, who had been on the lookout the whole time, approached the gentleman.

"My friends and I are on our way out," she whispered, as she discreetly slid her business card in his pocket. "If you don't get eaten alive, call me tomorrow," she added roguishly.

"I certainly will," smiled Aphroz. "You know what? I'd better go home now, too. If you don't mind, I'd like to leave this place by your side to avoid further hassle."

"Sure," agreed the charming lady with an amused smile playing on her lips. "I'm glad to act as your protector."

Outside, next to the cabs lined up in front of the Private Key, Aphroz exchanged a few words with Bibi before she left with her friends. He stood there, enjoying her lingering scent and the promise he read in her last look. But when he saw The Incandescent coming out of the club and walking resolutely toward him, he entered the nearest cab and quietly ordered, "Go!"

Chapter 8

The Journey

Could this be the end? Aphroz wondered as he sat at his desk, his business trapped in a downward spiral. Instead of reversing the trend, any of his decisions felt like pulling out a wooden stick in a game of Jenga, thus approaching the ineluctable fall of the tower. He could blame new competitors entering his industry with innovative products and massive means of corruption. But he saw neither the Linda-Marie danger nor the effects of his post-puritan chapter started on March 8, defined by another spiral —— a spiral of seduction, fed by itself, seemingly unstoppable and utterly distractive.

In the past, he had experienced many periods filled with romantic conquests. But ironically, this one derived from his love for one woman, Nady. To try to endure the yawning void felt in his chest when he could not go to Victoria, Aphroz would conquer other women, one after the other. But as a token of the dedication for which his heart yearned for Nady, he would do so at a frenetic pace, only to prevent anyone from becoming indispensable to him.

He would even let them know that his heart belongs to someone else to avoid other dramas and legitimate expectations. Oddly enough, the less involved he was, the more they wanted him and forgave his manufactured shortcomings. Each new love affair led to another without ending any. The gentleman had to save new contacts in his phone with additional details to avoid losing track.

Each of these women had something special. But since none could compare to Nady from Aphroz's point of view, they all contributed not only to uplifting the pedestal on which he had placed her but also to reinforcing his belief that he had found his perfect soulmate in her.

So, when the British embassy granted her a tourist visa, Aphroz was at a crossroads of professional uncertainties, multiple romances, the anonymous threat still looming over his head, and the possible fallout from the Kenzie and Hannah drama.

I've never seen so many women happy with the same man. (Building guard)

Nady returned from Victoria Thursday evening. Their flight to London via Nairobi was scheduled for the next day at 11:45 pm. On Friday morning, she asked Aphroz to accompany her to a suburban branch of her bank to withdraw cash.

"The sky is cloudy, why so far?" Aphroz asked.

"I need to see a friend," she answered quietly. "I will make it fast, but if you are busy…"

"No, darling, I can take you there despite the nightmarish traffic," Aphroz joked.

Aphroz waited outside in the car, while Nady entered the bank, carrying her sports bag like a tennis champion. She came out only one and a half hours later.

"Thank God you assured me you would be quick!" Aphroz teased.

"Sorry, baby. It was crowded, and it…"

"No worries, I am joking! But where is your sense of humor this morning?"

"Honestly, it will come back only after takeoff," Nady estimated.

"I know it's your first time flying, but don't worry about a thing."

"I feel like I'm going to forget to do a lot of things before we leave."

"Why bother, darling? We will only be away for two weeks."

Nady could only bestow a grim smile upon him. "Please drop me off at my mom's now. I must see my family before it starts to rain," she said.

A few minutes later, when he parked at the curb in front of her mother's place, Nady turned to him silently.

"Baby," she murmured.

"Yes, my love."

"Before our trip tonight, I want to let you know that I don't intend to come back to Cameroon," the young lady uttered.

Aphroz took his hands off the steering wheel, turning to Nady with a fierce gaze.

"Uh… What do you mean?"

She spoke softly. "As you know, I was born in a needy family, reliant on scraps my grandmother took home from European missionaries she worked for as a maid," Nady started. "I've been supporting my family for a long time, and I am very proud of it. After I was elected Miss Coca-Cola Cameroon, I believed I could do more for them. But due to shenanigans and corruption, I didn't receive the winner's prize initially included, neither the check nor the trip to Paris... Don't pity me, baby. I would have settled in France and could have helped my family, but I wouldn't have met you."

She paused, her fingers darting to the sides of Aphroz's head. He looked at her impassively. "Today, thanks to you," Nady continued, "I got a visa. Even though it's a tourist visa, I don't want to miss the opportunity to get out of this country. Do you understand? I must do everything in my power to break the chains of poverty that hold my family back. I am aware that wherever you go, you encounter hardships. But here, I don't see any opportunities for accomplishment peeking out from behind challenges. None."

Drops of rain splattered the windshield. Aphroz stared into Nady without seeing, only listening as her words fell. She shrank back into the seat, looking at him with the coquettish innocence of a woman afraid but possessed with certainty, and continued in a steady, deliberate tone.

"You are the most marvelous thing that has happened to me. I wish I could stop the flow of time and just savor these exceptional moments that we share. But I must confess, sometimes I fear that I'll wake up from this golden dream, withered and without your passion. I know you told me that I'll remain the most beautiful woman for the one who loves me, but who can predict life's circumstances?" She held his gaze and continued.

"I see how you struggle with your business and how you suffer from our local flaws —which, in my opinion, will eventually spoil your sophistication. If all this becomes unbearable and you don't want to lose the majesty in you that wins people's hearts, one of these days you may decide to leave for good. Your British passport gives you that option." She paused, reaching a tenuous moment.

"I love you with all my heart and my soul as I've never loved before. My most precious desire is to live by your side for the rest of my life in another country. I'd be delighted if you shared that dream. But feel no pressure. I don't expect an answer today. Just think about it."

Aphroz did not speak, only raising his eyebrows to show understanding. He sighed deeply, signaling nothing to Nady. She continued and spoke in a low but sweet voice, rising again to meet his inscrutable gaze.

"Your silence seems to hide secrets now...I like it when your eyes say you love me... I adore you too, baby. May you keep this smile, and may I be your eternal love... Kiss me." They kissed.

"I read in your face that you have something to tell me," Nady added. "And I also have one more thing to share with you, baby. But this weather looks bad. Let me go see my family. We'll talk later, okay? Kiss me again, love." She left in the steady drizzle, heading toward her family's home.

My husband is mad. I mean... crazy. (Koni)

In Cameroon, possibly more than anywhere else in the world, vanity drives people's attitudes. Those who hold prominent positions exude arrogance and study their body language to suggest even more power. Those who lack resounding titles affect —just with their gaze— to assume charges highly confidential as consequential. And those who have neither a business card nor public responsibilities pretend to have connections, granting them a free pass to act above the law. The longing to prove their importance or to see their awesomeness reflected in other people's eyes blindly crosses the boundaries of ridicule when it does not lead to the most unthinkable abuses.

Mr. E was no exception. Although air controllers have no outfits, he began wearing an aviator-style cap when he became a supervisor at the Douala Air Traffic Control Tower. He started a pre-shift routine. Every workday before heading to the control tower, he arrived early to walk around the terminal hall, counting the number of people who greeted him respectfully.

That Friday evening, the weather was terrible. However, with his chin up and chest swollen, thumbs in his waistband, he strode around the lobby and collected tributes to his importance from the eyes of the usual bystanders, employees, and vendors of the airport. At the end of the hall, which did not quite live up to the grandeur implied by the name Douala International Airport, his ego remained thirsty, as people were preoccupied by the wretched weather outside.

Since he had time on his hands, he entered the check-in area. It was filled only with travelers, and he positioned himself near the counters, visible to all. Seconds later, a traveler begged him to intervene with the attendant at the Kenya Airways counter about excess baggage. Mr. E's craving for reverence secretly exulted. He stepped closer as if he had authority in the matter, looked over the counter clerk's shoulder, and frowned disapprovingly at the traveler. Then with his index finger, he blatantly gestured "no favor" to the attendant.

He took pleasure in deceiving the bystanders, making them believe that he refrained from using his authority to help the traveler. After adjusting his pants and lifting his chin, he walked away with an air of heading toward more complex problems to solve. Just before exiting the check-in area, he discreetly looked at the crowd of travelers to gauge his effect... and his gaze picked out Aphroz, laughing at a joke from Nady.

In less than half a second of eye contact, Mr. E recognized his wife's lover, whom —until that very moment— he had only seen in pictures on Koni's phone. He suddenly whirled around and retraced his steps to the counter as if he had forgotten something important. A thorough examination of the passenger list left no doubt in his mind. The thought of his wife's lover being on the Kenya Airways flight rocked his head. It bounced around as he drove to the control tower under the heavy rain.

He likes her vulnerable strength. (MissLisa)

Nady was the first in her family to both travel overseas and board a plane. So, her entire clan, including cousins, aunts, and nieces gathered to bid her farewell. Boarding passes in hand, Aphroz and Nady joined her kinsfolk for a drink at the airport bar. Each individual harbored unique emotions, creating a strange mixture of sadness, pride, and jealousy in the atmosphere. Nevertheless, the beauty queen found the right words to infuse the occasion with soulfulness and smiles. She hugged everyone for the last time before departing, sobs shaking her solid frame and tears streaming down her face.

He certainly fell for her revolutionary spirit too. (CuttieKitty)

S tanding in the queue at the only police checkpoint, Aphroz discreetly pointed out to Nady the obvious nervousness of the traveler ahead of them.

"Look, his legs are trembling," he murmured.

"Do you think he's unwell?" Nady asked.

"He might have a fever, but it's more likely from fear than an actual illness."

"Fear?"

"He seems like a candidate for illegal immigration, possibly with a fake passport or visa, maybe even both."

"You really think so?"

"I'm certain of it. The anxiety of being caught even before boarding the plane is overwhelming him."

"You're probably right. He's shaking so much."

"By the time he reaches the border officer, he'll have sweated out all his fear. And when the first question is asked, he'll start stuttering."

"Oh!"

"I'm telling you. He lacks a plan to corrupt the agent, and at this point, that stands as his greatest adversity."

"How do you know?" Nady inquired.

"I've seen many people in this situation. I'll bet you a hundred to one he won't pass this check."

"Don't say that!"

"On the plane, you'll be able to spot the fraudsters by their fervent prayers. As soon as they sit down, they thank God."

"May God help this poor guy to be among them," Nady pleaded. "I know what happens to people who get rejected...Yes, I know. First, the authorities will detain him at the airport. And since he invested all his money in his passport and visa, he won't have anything left to buy his freedom from the Police Chief. They'll let him make a call. If none of his relatives can come with a huge bribe, they'll transfer him to Mbusa Mundi, our notorious welcome prison. He'll be there indefinitely. And believe it or not, sometimes Mbusa Mundi offers more benefits than one's dwelling. For, if your attempt at illegal immigration fails and you return to the gloomy neighbors you bid farewell to, you might become their laughingstock, which can lead to suicidal thoughts."

"I've encountered those kinds of people, baby," Aphroz murmured. "They endure their unfortunate situation by relishing the misfortune of others."

"This explains why some fraudsters prefer incognito imprisonment, so they can eventually emerge and pretend they've just returned from a trip. Don't smile, darling. It is so sad...It's terrible because those who try the adventure by sea or through the desert make a conscious choice to risk a horrible death rather than live in our country. And all this happens because France, with its colonial currency scam, robs us of our wealth and corrupts our leaders."

Nady's last words revealed her frustrated rebellion.

"You want my opinion?" she asked.

"I love it when you get passionate, sweetheart," Aphroz smiled.

"I'm not well-versed in politics, I confess. But to lift small nations out of the cycle of oppression and bad governance, naturalized immigrants should form an Immigrant Coalition in their Western host countries. This social movement would advocate for voting only for candidates committed to ending the effects and practices of imperialism worldwide. In my opinion, such an initiative would be a significant step towards creating a better world."

"Wow!" exclaimed Aphroz, filled with admiration. "And you claim to know nothing about politics."

"Smooth talker!"

"I'm thrilled when the spirit of revolution shines in your eyes," Aphroz whispered. "Your practicality, appropriateness, and intelligence enchant me. I love you so much, Nad."

"I adore you too, baby."

The queue moved forward. Before proceeding to the Border Officer, the traveler in front of them looked back at Nady as if he had been eavesdropping on their conversation all along and whispered, "Please pray for me."

They had to meet. (SissiKana)

Yep! It's a critical point in their respective lives, regardless of their future. (JollyJump)

T he boarding was supposed to start at 10:35 pm. Many passengers were already queuing up in front of the gate desk. However, the gate stood shut, with no hostess in sight, offering no clue as to the whereabouts of the plane. A long wait began for Aphroz and Nady.

From that enclosed departure lounge, which was not large enough to comfortably accommodate all passengers of one carrier, the outside of the airport was invisible. However, near the entrance, a glass partition on the top half of the wall showed the lobby leading to two other boarding areas further down. Occasionally, a few Kenya Airways agents would pass through that lobby, walking quietly, chatting, and laughing as colleagues do after a long workday. But they showed no indication of the urgency that the waiting passengers expected. Instead, they sometimes gazed at those travelers like second-hand items behind a discount store window.

Impatience at no sign of an impending boarding grew in the lounge and faces tensed up. People shook their heads in disbelief, breathing heavily to share their anger with their neighbors, and smirking to mean, "What a calamity, these African airlines!"

Unable to bear it any longer, a few angry women motivated themselves and stepped into the hallway, walking aggressively toward a passing Kenya Airways employee.

"What's going on?" they asked in unison.

Turning his head left and right, the airline employee —with a drawl that made one wonder if it was natural or fake— replied calmly, "What?"

"Are you serious?" shouted the most belligerent of the upset women. "The boarding for our flight should have started an hour and a half ago, and no one seems to care about us."

"But, ma'am, you must be aware of the storm outside, aren't you?"

"No, I'm not. You may not have noticed, but we can't see outside. How much will it cost you to officially inform us that the weather is delaying the operations?"

"There is no need to scream and even less to be hostile, ma'am."

"We've been waiting like idiots. Children are crying; they are hungry, thirsty, and sleepy. Do you care at all?"

"It's not my fault that this airport has neither an information screen nor adequate infrastructure for this kind of situation, ma'am."

"That's all?"

"Listen, ma'am. Go back to the departure lounge, take a seat, calm down, comfort the other passengers, and ask them to be patient..."

"You must be kidding! Is it my job to inform your customers?"

"Why not?" answered the pot-bellied agent as if he was telling a child, "You must be nice to your friends."

And he went away with his heavy step.

Nady and Aphroz remained seated, looking at each other and sharing a knowing smile. The pleasure of their companionship concealed the ticking of the clock, making the impatience around them seem as anecdotal as the subjects of their discussions so far.

"Sweetheart," Nady said as if she wanted to move on to a more substantial conversation. "This morning, you had something to tell me. What is it?"

"We'll talk about it in the plane," promised Aphroz.

"No way! Tell me now."

"In the plane."

"Have I shocked you with my decision?"

"Not at all, baby" whispered Aphroz. "It's something mysterious. We'll talk about it on the plane."

"Oh no! I'd rather be crucified on the ground than in the air. If you love me, tell me everything now."

"That's emotional blackmailing, Nad. Stop staring at me with that flirty look. Honey...honey, you're a naughty girl."

"I love you too, sweetheart."

"Okay! Here's the thing. I believe in the destiny of encounters. You know that. I don't consider myself superstitious, but I try to listen to Mother Nature and my instincts."

The gentleman took a deep breath before continuing.

"A few days ago, I had a dream about my father. His image and voice were clear as if he were standing right in front of me. I rarely have such vivid dreams. He spoke to me and gave me some advice, you know, like a father to his son. See what I mean? He wanted me to enjoy a happier married life than he did. He said that he could see how much my heart beats for you...yes...and he encouraged me to stop searching. I'm telling you... He said he knew we were destined for each other and that our love would flourish outside of Cameroon. In short, it seems like he was advising me to take you away from here."

Nady stood stunned. "You're joking!" she exclaimed.

"I told you it was incredible," Aphroz continued. "When I woke up, his words filled me up. They comforted me in the direction I wanted to take my existence. Though his advice solely existed in my dream, I intended to follow it, you know? It felt like a posthumous gift to make up for the emptiness of our relationship during his lifetime. When you told me of your plan this morning, I got goosebumps because I've been thinking of asking if you'd agree to live with me out of Cameroon."

"I get goosebumps right now, sweetheart," Nady breathed. "Why didn't you ask me?"

"I wanted to proceed in a certain order."

"Which is?"

"Go to London for vacation, come back home, and then..."

"No, baby. I don't want to come back here... I can't come back here."

How many people die yearly trying to emigrate to Europe? (Donald)
Guys, can we stay focused on Aphroz? (Popsico)

As they chatted, nervousness had increased significantly in the departure lounge. People now spoke loudly, while some travelers walked from one end of the room to the other, stretching or talking on their phones. The toddlers in their parents' arms were still awake and crying. A few young tourists in jeans sat on the floor, dozing on their duffel bags, while others lay unscrupulously on three-seater benches.

Amid the tension, Aphroz noticed many travelers gazing out through the half-glazed walls with as much curiosity as impatience. He got up and saw a dozen of police officers and military personnel of different ranks in the lobby. Four or five of them, with epaulets adorned with stars, marched proudly, their hands behind their backs, exuding a martial air. They seemed to struggle with a decision to make. The others, trying to compensate for their lower rank, clenched their jaws, glancing left and right as if to flush out a criminal, and held fiercely to the straps of their machine guns. Still, they had to adjust their pace to that of their superiors. Aphroz beckoned Nady to look. She got up, saw the squad of officers, and immediately slumped heavily into her chair.

"Are you alright, baby?" the gentleman asked, holding her hand.

"Uh... I...Yes. I don't know. I..."

"What's going on? Cat got your tongue?"

"I must confess something to you now, sweetheart," Nady finally spoke, her eyes staring off into the void.

"What is it?"

The young woman took a deep breath, gathering her thoughts.

"First of all, I want you to know that you are my present, my future, my happiness, my everything," she started as a preamble.

"Hmm, this sounds serious," Aphroz replied.

"Yes, it is. Listen, sweetheart. You didn't ask me any questions about the sports bag I took into the bank this morning or its contents when I came out. If you had asked, I don't know...anyway... Yesterday, at the end of my workday in Victoria, I credited my bank account with a substantial sum of money that did not belong to me."

The news stunned Aphroz, leaving his mouth gaping in amazement. He quickly looked around to make sure no one else had heard Nady's confession.

"Please, stay calm," she continued. "This morning, with the help of a former colleague, I withdrew the entire amount in cash at the branch you took me to... Yes, I filled the bag with that stolen money. I left half of it to my family. I didn't want to involve you in this. No, I really didn't ...And just two minutes ago, I would have said that I'm not worried because, according to my calculations, the bank won't find out until Tuesday. I know when and how they perform the accounting reconciliation."

"And...now?" Aphroz asked calmly.

"At this very moment, I'm not sure of anything," admitted the young woman. "Seeing all these policemen makes me doubt. I'm afraid they're after me. Maybe I forgot a detail."

Feeling more dead than alive, she rested her head on Aphroz's lap like a little girl, utterly weary. Aphroz closed his eyes, allowing his mind to absorb the situation. He gently patted her shoulder with one hand while massaging his forehead with the other. Their consciousness filtered the surrounding noises and nervousness, allowing them to perceive the movement of the men in uniform —approach, stopping, moving away, coming back.

In the secret of her imagination, Nady could already see those soldiers barging in, their machine guns pointed at her, with strong arms lifting her as if she were a safari prize. She agreed with herself that she wouldn't provoke their overzealousness with handcuffing resistance or false air of incomprehension. Nor would she seek martyrdom by crying out shrilly. Instead, she would try to keep the dignified attitude of one who surrenders to an adverse fate, even though she currently felt more ashamed than the fraudster who had been arrested earlier at the checkpoint. There were far too many officers for her to consider corrupting all of them. But what if she tried to bribe only their leader? The thought floated enticingly through her mind. Yes, just the chief... The idea comforted her soul enough to keep it from absolute despair.

As if a similar idea had crossed Aphroz's mind at the same time, he straightened. The commotion had intensified both inside and outside the boarding room. The gentleman cocked his head to watch outside. Kenya Airways officials and police officers were engaged in a heated discussion, but their exchange, which was obscured by the closed door, remained indecipherable. Several armed guards were now stationed in front of the lounge entrance while others paced as loudly as possible with the apparent satisfaction of sowing questions in the mind of travelers. One policeman opened the door of the lounge and asked loudly, "Here, Chief?"

"Yes," someone replied.

Nady flinched. "Let it be according to your will, My Lord," she prayed. Then she sat up, holding Aphroz's hand tightly.

"I love you and I am with you," Aphroz whispered confidentially.

Three tall soldiers strode in, commanding standers to clear the way from the entrance to the gate. The soldiers' steely gaze dissuaded some hesitant travelers from resisting, and the men in uniform stood stiffly on this passage after an exchange of odd signs with the rest of the squad outside. Then, a Kenya Airways hostess entered the lounge.

"Can we at least know what's going on this time?" a traveler with a British accent shouted exhaustedly.

"A flood in the VIP lounge compels us to use this gate for the Minister of Infrastructure," answered the hostess, triggering a storm of hisses and rolling eyes.

Aphroz and Nady looked at each other and exhaled deeply as if they had been holding their breath the whole time.

The more I think about it, the more I want you to call me El Don from now on. (Donald) *LOL!* (MouMouss)

Once the Minister was seated on the plane, there was a prolonged delay before general boarding could begin. And after the boarding, which was completed in an atmosphere full of travelers' anger, another waiting period began in the plane due to the raging storm over Douala.

At the control tour, Mr. E scanned the darkness with his infrared binoculars. He had never experienced such horrific conditions, worsening over time. A fire truck struggled to inspect the runway, while on the adjacent wasteland, long grasses swayed in a wild ballet orchestrated by the wind. Trees in the distance thrashed from side to side. Further to the left, the corrugated iron roofs of a few nearby houses ripped off and crashed against the airport security fence.

Mr. E glared blankly, his mind filled with hatred toward Aphroz. Their eye contact in the check-in area revived painful memories. The images from the Red File and numerous impure thoughts swirled around his head. The family words that had convinced him at the time not to repudiate Koni now haunted him, layering humiliation upon his rancor, as if the events were unfolding anew.

By exposing his wife's intimacy to family and guests, he intended to shame her before throwing her out like a used rag. However, his final decision not to separate from her had dashed embarrassment against him. Yaoundé's assignment had provided a lifeline that he would have preferred to keep, and returning to Douala was not his preference, but the promotion's allure overpowered his hesitation.

Had he met Aphroz's gaze elsewhere, he likely would have been less disturbed by the resurgence of those memories. But his ego could not swallow the affront of seeing that smiling face inside the airport, where people respectfully address him as "Mr. Air Traffic Supervisor". The deranged man, erupting inwardly, trembled from head to toe, his hunger for retaliation echoing the fury of the raging elements. As he watched their effects through his binoculars with growing fascination, an unsettling idea crept into his mind and took hold: the only possible revenge was to hurl Aphroz into the fury of nature.

No sooner had he pictured the conclusion than the intercom buzzed. The two controllers seated behind him later reported that when Mr. E turned around, he panted like a pig. He tried to gather his wits, wiping his sweaty forehead before pressing the flashing button.

"AT. Supervisor speaking," he answered.

"Hello, dear! This is Chief Onana of the Border Police speaking."

"Evening, sir. You're on speaker. I'm surprised to hear your voice."

"I'm standing here with the Governor, who has something to tell you. Hold on."

"Mr. Supervisor, The Governor speaking."

"Mr. Governor..."

"Alright, I understand that we have terrible weather conditions, and you are overseeing everything as it should be. However, the Minister of Infrastructure is on flight 507 of Kenya Airways. Do you follow?"

"Yes, sir," answered Mr. E, still panting.

"Some circumstances require the Minister to travel tonight. It would be highly appreciated if you could expedite the departure of his flight."

Mr. E's face brightened as if he were watching a missing piece of a puzzle fall demonically into place. He turned to the young controllers to ensure they heard what could be considered a directive from higher-ups. They nodded.

"You can count on me, Your Excellency," he promised.

Should we include all our findings in the report? (SissiKana)

While waiting, Aphroz and Nady entertained themselves with conversations, cuddling, and playful teasing.

"Why are you recording our conversations on your phone?" Aphroz asked.

"It's a habit I picked up since Victoria. It allowed me to listen to your voice again when you were gone. And now, I can't help but hit the record button as soon as we start talking. I hope you don't mind."

"No, it's okay."

"So, how did you feel earlier when officers burst into the gate room?" the young lady asked.

Aphroz smiled calmly.

"I was as stressed as I was during the rocky situation that followed my childhood adventure with Solange."

"That's so funny! The girl when you were eight?"

"Yes."

"Tell me more! What happened after you rolled in the hay or rather in the stairs?"

Aphroz laughed.

"After our little business, we parted ways," he recounted. "She ran to her house, farther down the alley that bordered our residence. As for me, instead of going up to the third floor at my biological mother's, where I spent my vacations with my grandmother, I couldn't resist going down to the first floor and boasting about my adult adventure to my friends, the Foudazib brothers. As I've told you, they had left the game of hide and seek at dinner time. You remember?"

"I do. So, what did you tell them?"

"I recounted the coitus, but they didn't believe me until I gave details and showed them exhibit number one, still tainted by Solange's intimacy."

"Oh, my goodness! You did?"

"Yeah! Otherwise, they wouldn't let me peep in the keyhole of their parents as they used to."

"Oh my..."

"I probably shouldn't be telling you this kind of stuff."

"You were a kid. Tell me everything."

"You should have seen my friends, eyes wide open with curiosity and envy at the same time. I felt immense pride as I watched them drool with jealousy. But less than twenty-four hours later, vanity taught me its expense."

"What happened?" Nady asked impatiently.

"The next afternoon, I was on our balcony, reading a comic next to my grandmother sewing and my mother manicuring herself, when a growing crowd noise drew our attention. It sounded like an argument between two children, fanned by other children eager for a fight. That was not unusual in our neighborhood. I stood up and watched in the direction of those voices. They were coming from the alley leading to Solange's family villa. The company approached, the noise grew, and I looked forward to seeing this show from our balcony. As I started to recognize my pals from afar among the crowd, Grandma asked me, 'Isn't that your name they chant so nervously?' That's when I listened attentively and heard, 'Aphroz, you'll get a sound thrashing! Aphroz, you'll get a lifetime beating!'

"Oh, ho!" Nady exclaimed.

"Yeah! And it confused me even more when I saw Solange, fiercer than ever, leading this frenzied crowd made up of our usual friends, including the Foudazibs and a few teenagers from who knows where. I'm telling you, the happenings were a mystery to me, but their virulent chants gave birth to silent anguish in me."

"What about your mom and grandma?" Nady asked.

"By that time, Grandma had heard my name, but she didn't catch the chant. She impatiently dismissed me, 'Go play with your friends before they disturb our neighbors.' So, I ran down the stairs, out of our residence, and into the alley to meet that mob."

"Not afraid?"

"Afraid? No. As a boy, I avoided trouble and feared nothing. Curious and surprised? Yes. I simply wanted to find out why they chanted my name threateningly. When they saw me coming toward them, their chants increased in intensity. About a dozen people were jumping around, shouting, predicting an extraordinary beating from my mother, and looking forward to that hilarious spectacle. Some of them had already prepared huge wood sticks for my butt. Joining them didn't stop their progress toward our building. Solange scowled angrily, her silence unbroken amidst the others. So, as I was now walking with this loud group of kids toward my place, I came close to her."

"What's happening?" I asked her in a hushed tone.

"I'm going to see your mom and complain to her that you're spreading the rumor of having screwed me," she whispered with resentment.

"But…"

"You shouldn't have mentioned it to anybody. Now, they're all making fun of me," Solange murmured angrily.

"P…Please, don't tell my mom," I begged.

"Sorry, but I must. Otherwise, they'll keep calling me Solange-the-Slut."

"What… What exactly are you going to say?" I asked.

"That you're pretending to have effed me."

"Are you going to use that "F" word in front of my mother?"

"Yes," Solange answered with a naive tone.

"My mom will kill me."

"She shrugged," Aphroz recalled. "I was petrified, Nad. Feeling as if the entire world was about to vanish under my feet. And, to answer your question, that's exactly what I felt earlier in the departure lounge."

"I see," Nady uttered in a barely audible whisper. "I'm sorry to have put you in that situation, honey."

"It's okay."

"What happened next with Solange?" Nady asked.

The gentleman sat up and smiled pensively.

"The noisy mob entered the gate of our residence," he recalled. "The situation, including the guys' colorful way of speculating on my fate had already numbed me. Most of those boys were taller and stronger than me. I started praying, 'Dear Little Jesus, I've done well in school lately. I brought home an excellent report card. Today I've been an excellent boy, I've done all my homework and all the chores Grandma asked me to do. Please, Lord, keep that in mind when you judge me. I admit, I shouldn't have boasted about my… sexual activity. But I promise, if you don't abandon me this time, I will keep my mouth shut in the future. O Almighty, save me."

"No kidding! You really prayed to Jesus like that?" Nady laughed. "Why you called him *Little*?"

"With grandma's stories, I believed that God's son was in charge of the kids and was as old as me."

The lovers didn't care about the passing of time or the tempestuous weather outside. They didn't even notice that the aircraft had started to maneuver toward the runway.

"Then, what happened?" Nady asked.

"We all climbed the staircase, with the mob shouting behind Solange and me. I was horrified, thinking of the moment Solange would use the 'F' word about me in front of my mother. But I couldn't climb the stairs any slower than this hostile crowd pushing me around. We were halfway to our floor when Grandma suddenly appeared above us, holding a long broomstick, her face purposely wearing a fierce look. From the balcony, she had seen and attributed my distress to this gang. She thundered louder than the uproar, pulled Solange and me behind her, and started twirling the broomstick menacingly over the crowd. 'Y'all get the hell out of here!' she shouted, chasing them. And they all fled."

"Why did your grandma protect Solange?" Nady asked.

"Because she knew her. Solange had come to my place a couple of times before."

"Hm!"

"Are you jealous?"

"Yes, I am... even though you were a child then."

"I love you too, Nad. And I'm jealous of all the men on whom you've bestowed your gaze before me."

Aphroz laughed.

"Don't flatter me, naughty boy. Tell me what happened next."

"After Grandma got rid of that herd of haters, Solange told her she wanted to see my mother. I wasn't out of the woods yet. We walked into our apartment and headed out to the balcony. I looked at Solange, and the determination on her face reminded me of the 'F' word. I would have peed in my pants without even knowing, but I quickly prayed again.

"My mother, unfazed, was methodically putting on nail polish.

"She welcomed Solange. 'How are you, sweetie?'

'I'm fine, Aunty. I just...'

'What's happening?'

"Solange awkwardly twisted her fingers and her body in all directions before contorting her brows into a serious expression when my mother looked up at her. Then she pouted and said, 'Aphroz is telling everybody that he...that he has... That we...that I am his wife.'"

Nady burst out into uncontrollable laughter for a whole minute, drawing the attention of many travelers.

"No F word?" she asked.

"No. No F word. And my mother replied, 'He said you're his wife, so what, honey? Don't you often have fun together? Don't mind what the other kids are saying. They are just jealous of you. Why don't you go and have a snack in the kitchen?'

"And my ordeal ended," concluded Aphroz.

The aircraft waited at the end of the runway, its wings visibly shaken by the violence of the elements. Its engine roared, and after an unusually long and unstable ride on the runway, it took off. To dispel the nostalgia that had taken hold of her, along with the anxiety of altitude, Nady resumed the conversation after a silent prayer.

"So how did you feel when the dreaded word did not come out from Solange's mouth?" she asked.

"It's hard to describe, but I was reborn and freed from the weight of vanity."

"You little rascal!"

Nady laughed again, but her face suddenly became an atrocious grimace as shouts arose from everywhere. The aircraft ascending brutally tilted up and on the right side in several attempts to straighten up, but it tilted multiple times as if the pilot gave opposite commands alternatively. Lights blinked everywhere, and people screaming wildly. Like a roller coaster ride, the plane plunged and nose-dived, amidst deafening cries of terror.

The realization of an inescapable end dawned upon Nady and Aphroz simultaneously. Breathless and holding hands, they tightened their embrace.

"Sweetheart!" cried the young woman, her voice trembling with the vibrations of all the love she wished to convey to the man of her life.

"I love you forever," Aphroz shouted.

The next moment, the aircraft crashed on the ground. One minute and forty-two seconds after takeoff.

[DEAR READER, I DOUBLE-CHECKED THE CRASH OF KENYA AIRWAYS FLIGHT 507, NOT OUT OF MORBID VOYEURISM. I PRAYED FOR IT TO BE FALSE. ITS VERACITY DEALT A DEVASTATING BLOW. TO QUOTE MRS. McGOVERN-GILL, "UNFORTUNATELY, THAT'S HOW LIFE GOES."]

Chapter 9

Farewell

When we were young, he had such a fascinating personality that one day I said, 'I want to be you'. He laughed. I remember it as if it were yesterday. (Babo)

In the garden of their estate, where the two cousins have hosted joyful barbecues, friends and families of Nady and Aphroz sat, all dressed in black mourning attire. Kooz found Nady's mom, who had agreed to a joint funeral ceremony, after seeing the unbearable images of the disaster broadcast on TV. The images showed two burnt hands interlaced, each wearing a copper and gold bracelet. Those twin bracelets made their identification possible, as Nady had proudly shown this gift from Aphroz to her mother on the day of their trip.

Aphroz's mourners were mostly women who shared a common quality: gorgeousness. They differed from each other in terms of age and style, but they all competed for elegance as if seeking the ultimate compliment from Aphroz and marking his farewell with the seal of seduction. Their glamour transformed the funeral ceremony into a scene reminiscent of a high-end fashion magazine photo shoot, even as they gently wiped away tears concealed beneath their sunglasses. No shouting, no frantic gesticulation. No loud mourning, no excessive sadness. Just elegance.

Ravel's concerto in G major, which Aphroz loved so much, played. Kooz listened as if secrets were hidden between the notes. His pale, sallow face suggested he hadn't been eating properly for three weeks. Struggling from behind the podium, he fixed his gaze on the wounded audience, staggered, and nearly fainted. Tim, his elder son, swiftly grabbed him and helped him sit to the side. Realizing that his father couldn't deliver Aphroz's eulogy, Tim scanned the crowd and decided to take the stage.

"Good afternoon," he started. "May peace be with you."

"And with you too," murmured the crowd.

"The tragic demise of my beloved uncle Aphroz has plunged our hearts into an overwhelming abyss of sadness and grief, as you can imagine. I would like to thank you all for your presence and…"

"Tim," Kooz called out with a weak voice.

Tim knelt to his father. Kooz spoke briefly, took some folded sheets of paper from his pocket, and handed them to his son with a trembling hand. As Tim returned to the podium, tears welled up in his eyes. With a momentary pause to collect himself, he continued his speech, struggling to steady his voice.

"I was not prepared to address you, and certainly not this way. But, as many of you know, my uncle Aphroz was a man with an unwavering passion for poetry. He had left behind a legacy that transcended his untimely departure. We found on his desk what we believe to be his final poetic creation."

Tim could not control his sob as he unfolded the sheets of paper, turning away from the microphone to recover his composure. He wiped away his tears before resuming his speech.

"I have the sad privilege…of discovering it…while reading it to you. My uncle titled it 'Ladies'."

The young man cleared his throat.

"Ladies,

Before the time ticking away hide what is true,
Let me kowtow to The Heaven, Mankind, and You,
Naked but draped in my conscience and thoughtfulness,
To put my life on the spot, repent and confess.

I have loved without measure
and counted neither the flowers
nor the hours.
I have sought pleasure
and accepted pains
and strains
I have loved despite dangers,
Looming from many corners.

I stole hearts
To savor flesh,
I crushed quartz
To start afresh.
But I assure,
My love was pure.

Shall the afterglow taste bitter
Or your memory just litter,
Then, you've missed the divine moment
When my life was in your weak hand.
Oh Yes! Dear, you held my destiny
At least for a brief eternity.

Remember me, shall you,
As a simple man
Or a gentleman,
Who made sacrifices
But no vain promises,
And lost many resources
For the sake of love forces,
Who explored ardor
Far beyond glamour
And traveled it with you
Detour after detour.

I always gave you my full me.
Sometimes, after controversy,
And inertia,
I have decided to step back,
With no animosity. But,
When I reclaimed my heart, despite tears,
I offered my body, despite fears.
And vice versa.

Now that the sun sets
I have no regrets.
I'd exchange thousands of past soreness
for one moment of our happiness.
May the universe bear witness
To the mysteries
Of our love stories.

On Judgment Day,
Without batting an eye,
Without trying to lie,
I'll tell Yahweh,
'Father, I loved every one of them,
I cherished every lady,
And my heart stopped on one precious gem,
Her mother calls her Nady."

Epilogue

B eloved reader, amid the peculiarity of this funeral, something even more unusual happened. Its details were not among Mrs. McGovern-Gill's students' findings when their work stopped reaching me. I'm proud to have discovered that information by directly communicating through emails with some women present at the time. They told me that after Tim finished reading Aphroz's last poem, all the ladies sitting in the "Aphroz's Friends" section of mourners realized their connection. They had each held a similar and yet special place in Aphroz's life at one point. Except for Kenzie and Hannah, none of them knew each other. However, they felt transported by a strange surge of sympathy, which they couldn't help but yield to, as if an invisible force were taking over them. They turned around, stood up, and consoled each other, their faces reflecting a blend of empathy, emptiness, and sorrow.

The spectacle of six dozen women all dressed in black, hugging each other in silence, lasted about an hour. Some speculated that Aphroz, from up above, had orchestrated the surreal scene. Indeed, eight of those ladies separately confided in me, each expressing her hesitance to sound irrational, and revealed that during the collective hugging moment, the gentleman appeared in one corner of the tent. They saw him standing and gazing at them. He smiled, sent a kiss through his fingers, and disappeared.

As a believer in life after death, I have no reason to doubt their accounts. I would have liked to quote their full testimony, but I must leave you here, dear reader. I have to run if I don't want to keep Leslie waiting. In a few minutes, she will join me in our long-time secret hideout, her husband having gone fishing with friends in a new boat. It's puzzling how she frequently mentions her husband or exes, but never Aphroz. Should I bring him up to her?

END

Dear reader,

*If you enjoyed reading this book, consider posting a wonderful review in your preferred media without revealing the ending.
I appreciate your feedback. It is imperative to my writing.
Thank you.*

Alexis Eyondi

Books by
ALEXIS EYONDI

<u>Mr. K's Decision</u>

"Should someone call me now to announce her death, I wouldn't even blink, let alone attend her funeral."

If a mother's love knows no bounds, how has Mr. K come to forsake the woman who gave him life? Maybe a secret locked behind tight lips finally escaped.

Stunned by his decision, the evening guests of Tiffany Estate turned into eager listeners of a story that should have been straightforward. Yet, as his narration of damaged family ties reveals a seemingly never-ending path of shame, opposition among the crowd lends favor for and against Mr. K. But can the guests maintain their black and white stances as the tale becomes more intricate? And does the saying, 'A mother's love is infinite', truly apply to all mothers?

<u>Les Sournoiseries De Gens Respectables</u>

(Inspiré d'une histoire terriblement vraie). Il y a une foule nombreuse et tout le monde rivalise d'élégance, d'abord parce que ce sont des obsèques, ensuite parce que la défunte était de noble naissance. Une rumeur silencieuse incrimine le veuf de cette mort sans effusion de sang. Il faut bien admettre qu'ici à GossaCity, le commérage est une discipline mondaine. Mais, pour une fois, de l'aveu même de la défunte, le bruit semble être fondé : « Il me tuera, c'est fatal » avait-elle confié à sa domestique. Pourquoi cette sombre prophétie ? Était-ce la révélation que les perfidies de son époux, mêlées d'une féroce avidité, demeuraient à ce point vengeresses, qu'elles ne pouvaient se conclurent qu'en apothéose funeste ? La moitié de la réponse est courbée au-dessus du tombeau. Ceux qui l'observent le plus sont des survivants de l'affaire qui agita les esprits à Paris et Toulouse, avant d'opposer ici la famille du veuf à celle de la défunte. Une rixe mémorable. [Après avoir entraîné le lecteur dans les arcanes de quelques esprits sournois chargés de cupidité, de haine ou de fatuité, l'auteur le défie de retrouver les traces et les noms des protagonistes de cette histoire.]

L'Instinct De Séduction (Muna Jomboss)

Tandis qu'à GossaCity ses petits camarades s'émerveillaient devant les voitures miniatures, Aphroz n'avait d'yeux que pour les courbes féminines matures… Qu'on ne s'y trompe pas, tous les garçons en culotte courte ne rêvent pas de devenir pilotes de course. De temps en temps, au milieu de l'inattendu, certains parmi eux sont mystérieusement touchés par une fantaisie de la providence ou un génie quelconque. À cinq ans, Mozart créa sa première composition musicale, n'est-ce pas ? Eh bien, au même âge, beaucoup plus près de nous, sans savoir qu'il avait de la séduction une compréhension viscérale, Aphroz prit la décision de sa vie : « Quand je serai grand, je serai séducteur ». Sa nature venait de lui être révélée… La passion des femmes était inscrite en nobles caractères dans ses gènes… En voici le trajet.

La Décision De Monsieur K

On en est au digestif, à la fin d'une réception mondaine qui réunit à New York des gens du monde des affaires, de la diplomatie onusienne et de la francophonie ; les échanges sont feutrés, les esprits pétillent. Soudain, une animation inattendue monte d'une des tables : Monsieur K, un des convives, vient de déclarer en toute tranquillité qu'il n'assisterait pas aux obsèques de sa propre mère, si jamais elle venait à décéder. Bientôt, ce gentleman doit affronter l'émoi des deux cents invités agglomérés autour de lui, scandalisés… mais qui consentent à écouter les détails d'une histoire qui entraîne le lecteur des années 60 à nos jours et de la France aux Etats-Unis en passant par le Cameroun. Ses arguments auront-ils raison des principes de cette honorable assemblée ou inversement ?

www.ingramcontent.com/pod-product-compliance
Lightning Source LLC
Chambersburg PA
CBHW020624160726
47991CB00002BA/924